The Boil

R L Alana

ISBNs
Paperback: 978-1-80227-272-7
eBook: 978-1-80227-271-0

Table of Contents

Acknowledgement

To my muses and inspirations,
Abigail O and Laura S

Chapter 1.
Water of Life

That morning, Christopher Myen heard the songs of two pitta birds as they screeched with satisfaction. He picked up their jubilance as they fluttered between branches; he heard the symphony of tweets and toots and made the astonishing observation that both pittas had been in his dreams the night before when he'd fallen under the influence of a draw of a north-eastern harvest of Indian hallucinogen. The pittas' song halted for a moment, and he allowed himself the pleasure of witnessing the sun breaking out of the horizon of orange clouds. He knew the pittas had stopped either to rest or indulge in their vocation of worm picking from the dirt hidden beneath the autumn drop of golden leaves from the ginkgo tree that stood majestically outside his window.

Christopher recollected moments of celebration lasting long into the night and the sound of a few chattering below; he'd recognised his mother's voice amongst them. He was still half asleep, with the remedies of acetaminophen working through his inner linings and numbing his stomach. It had been his tenth celebration of life, and it was also the first time the woman of distortion had appeared to him at night. She was as fluid as his dreams and as sustained as water crashing over the fall from which he viewed the world. She had gifted him with a kiss and spoken in a very reassuring way, not as mothers do to their young but more as lovers do. You will remember this, she said and left a cold imprint on his lips, a slick of saliva as cool as mentha that lasted long after she had thrown his mind and disappeared into a mist in his dreams.

Kamari the Bombay pushed past the frolic of shadows that hindered, making its body lean so it could pass through the gap in the door, and created an audience with Christopher, in a world of his own lucid wandering. It rubbed its back against the wood to outbid the lingering scent of old rose in a vase of aged lavender water that had built up in the room.

Well… goodness me, I thought you did been dead, Kamari said. I have been stood out there long enough for four summers and a winter of harsh temperament to pass, banging my head on the door so that the whole neighbourhood could hear my rage at you. Casper is way past tending to, his hooves gone to mush, and Old Major isn't too pleased he isn't getting his straw from the batch of fine barley.

When Christopher finally got out of bed, it was with a sweat-dripped torso of molasses, his undergarment soaked in a long-condoned cocktail of his own bodily fluid that whiffed up his nostrils faster than a steam of pot release. The rush of what had happened the night before paid him a visit, a gentle reminder that all had, in fact, been an instance as real as the very count of his age of ten, simmering with notions of young adolescence and yearnings for flight, the same ones that had gotten boys of that age to don capes out of bedsheets and hover on the verge of death.

At some point we must have levitated, Christopher thought, oblivious of the Bombay being in great haste to get to lower ground. He dealt with the incessant thoughts that ran around in his head – market places where flower merchants sold pots of plants and autumn flowers like dope to young impressionable spinsters, and faces of strangers, including the woman he recognised, but he was unsure whether he had, indeed, known her. She was of a certain age and had a certain aura, that of a majestic thoroughbred, strides the size of thunder and an appearance that got much attention, even if men didn't want to look for dismal fear that she would be truly out of reach.

When Christopher's presence returned to his room it was with an acute stillness. He watched the Bombay brush against the radiator as it always did in the morning and jump on top of the TV set. It marked its territory with urine when it got annoyed or wanted a firm stroke of attention from him. He heard Kamari say in its frivolous way, I am past tending, too. The hunger it harboured burned a sulphuric hole in its belly and was of no use to anyone except to raise hell from the pit of doom itself. You seem to have fallen into yet another one, the Bombay said, and exited with its tail high up in the air and dancing the bolingo.

When the state of absolute docility receded, Christopher listened to the glorious chorus of tweets and toots from the pittas making their last call, as though to summon him from the depths of slumber. Their sharp, coarse calls tugged at him from such a depth that they unsteadied him and caused him to knock his big toe against the wooden leg of the bed. With his eyes fixated on the basin, he made his way to a mercury mirror hanging above it, ruined with blemishes.

Christopher lost himself in the mirror yet again to another world of wonders and likened the intensity of his pain to a hit of methamphetamine. He weighed up images of himself in the mirror, haggard as the Old Major, yet visceral in mind as a youth of ten.

Milliseconds, he thought. That's all it takes to get away in your head. He allowed the cold tap to run loose and watched the pour of water as though witnessing punitive cleansing. The Old Major's lodge is a good 15 minutes away, three at a pace, he thought.

You owe me a day's work, he heard the voice of the Old Major intrude into his reasoning. I insisted for days. You were unable to clean out my hooves and rid my stable of horse flies. What a mess. Now I am nearer to death, and my feed is no more appealing than a dung pile, he heard the Old Major neigh into the mist.

Christopher took up the mapping of his room, where dusk had abandoned the voyage of shadows, where they had danced and where they had hardly mimicked them. He set his eyes on the cracks in his walls, exactly as he had seen them in his dreams, and the growth of mould, exactly as he had seen it, present and giving off gases. He took the gentle water and applied it to his face, assured that the coldness would make him shiver. Then, he recounted the multiple why's in his head and debated them as gamblers do to a fault.

Chapter 2.
The Birth of Nonsensical

A brief moment passed in Christopher's ascent of the stairway that led to a glimmer of light. He took on his consciousness and measured up the old stairway before him; the height of the steps and the variance of levels were distorted and unfamiliar. He employed his youthful strength and balanced himself, listening out for the long-dreaded creak as he stepped. This time, the complaints of infested wood came slowly to his ears. When he eventually heard them, they were louder than before, as though a common beetle had feasted longer so the wood had become more of a hollow than a fine construct of interwoven carbon.

Christopher walked into his room and fell to the ground, his logic scattered like pieces of possessions about the floor. When he rose to his feet, it was to proclaim to himself that the thoroughbred needed feeding and with a sudden epiphany that all in the world was, like a child's birth, absolutely nonsensical.

He woke a third time to find himself walking a busy street of pedestrian traffic. The locale was lined with scores of second-hand thrifts, loaded with a portioned generosity of pilgrim business, steeped in the greed of high-end palaver and the occasional passing of pets that looked like their human owners. It seemed to him that the animals held more composure than their human owners with the way the canines pulled their humans along, almost to the point of falling.

He saw the face of the woman this time, different from the previous way she had presented herself to him. He saw her in the midst of busy comings and goings, dressed in white like the petals of thorns that broke and set her aside like an outsider in a crowd. He witnessed her coyness as she strolled like a lamb in the midst of wolves, bashfully avoiding the gaze of men of cooperative sentiment, although none took note of her, her waltz or her poor choice of garment of easy stain, cherry-picking her way through the crowd like a bride in white.

Myen knew she was the woman, the one from his dreams, there alone with her dance of untamed manner and her way of making things come alive with a single note, high in pitch and nurtured in careless groans of boundless pleasure. It had made the porcelains become still in their bizarre movements when the night was as bright as steel and his room was ablaze as daylight itself and all as a result of the quartz of her eyes.

She drifted through the crowd, rather than with it. Myen sensed the arrested spirit of the woman, captivating as a king sundew to prowling insects. It was as though she was the same woman but of different form, like the same person seen in a different light, like when lost love is longed for but seen around every corner in the faces of different people or heard in the accent of an enquiring tourist.

She brushed through his daydreams, pursuing a good fight like a Boris. She weighed up her manners as she teased him with a glance as she passed him in the street, which let on to him that this wasn't a dream but real life, as real as he could make it, as real as the beating of the heart in his chest.

Myen recounted with conviction the many faces that came and went in his dreams. The woman had been the one that stood out the most, but why, he questioned himself. It could only have been in his dreams, there alone recurring like a metronome in his sleep.

He felt his eyes tingling and saw the afterglow of a kick from a dose that had put him in a daze. He carried a smile of sneaked satisfaction on his face and suddenly came upon a meaning of life which flitted away from him like the wind. Did you miss me? came the voice of one Christina DeSilva doing a ritual dance about his loft room, running parameters of hallucinogens and baked in the high-salt sweat of an exhausted soul reaching for an ounce of stamina as for a biscuit from a jar.

Breaking me is something, but did you miss me? she asked. Christopher Myen spun a web of kaleidoscope in his mind, visions of depleted mercury making everything blurry. Chords of the music of his band lingered in the distance like liquorice on his tongue, the music of one Miles Dewey Davis III, composed as raw as the barley straw he watched the thoroughbred chew on early in the mornings. Its defecation was something of an electric discharge, bringing the clarity that even the most brilliant needed the junk to survive.

You worry too much, to excess, Christina DeSilva said. It will do you no good. Come with me – we can count the stars like we used to, together, same as we've always done, she urged. We flew once before like the two pittas – do you remember them? she asked. Oh, such a shame that you carry the weight of the world around with you! It's eating away at you. The world's weight on your shoulders... Regardless of what you do, it will stew away like a pot on a stove in a kitchen, and the more you think it over, the more it eats at you. You give it heat, like a pot on a stove in a kitchen, boiling away into mist.

Chapter 3.
The Boil

Christopher Myen's Boil was comprised of a gran cassa bass drummer, Ayer Frederickson, a Steinway & Sons grand pianist, Chiyoko Matsukawa, an Ibanez double bassist, Sebastian Evans, and himself. Christopher Myen handled a Stradivarius Bach piccolo Bb trumpet with sheer genius.

Their noise continued to make no sense, and their incoherency irritated him. He had measured it up and deemed it worse than scratches being made on a board. It had caused a gentle rumble to build in his lower abdomen that he also measured up and deemed worse than a deprived baby's craving for mother's milk.

The conversations of men in dim rooms entered into his subconscious. The two men wore their beards long and bulky as ginger nodes, and their eyes were as acute as those of the Bombay cat. Both had struggled to keep a good growth of hair, but it fell out from their scalps as quickly as it regrew until it receded like waves at low tide and left a shiny glow where the hair follicles would have been. In their midst, Christopher Myen saw the redhead with flames like an alatus plant. He noticed how quickly she adjusted and became even more alluring than when he had played solo to her in the vacancies of persuasion.

She spoke very little, and the two men hung on her every word. I've never heard anything so unique before, she said, as to control music with their minds, she added and burst into laughter. The two naturally joined in and anchored on a counterfeit version of their own laughter.

Christopher pondered the validity of what he'd witnessed. The same woman had gotten up and offered a clap when their incoherency of noise had stopped; the room joined in, and naturally, they brought the show to a close with a thunder of applause.

The night before, they had played like gods, the lady with hair like an alatus had said, to ignite the low burn of lustful desire she sensed in his loins and in his sweat that oozed raw musk and in the strength with which he handled his piccolo Bb and waved it about like a beacon of true passion.

Christopher took a sweep around the room and saw that his audience were in awe; gapes had replaced closed lips, and all seemed to harbour a boiling confusion about what they had just witnessed. He allowed the grace of the passing moment to soak in and, in his usual manner, nodded to his band mates. Chiyoko Matsukawa on piano, he said, watching the gentle build-up of applause from the crowd; Ayeh Frederickson on drums… Sebastian Evans on bass… and finally, myself,

Christopher Myen on trumpet. These are my band mates, Christopher said, engulfed in a ball of gleeful joy, basking in the triumph that they had just created from patience.

We thank you for joining us tonight, Christopher said. Thank you, he added with a nod to the crowd. We hope you've all enjoyed our playing tonight. Christopher clocked numbers in his head of the crowd: forty-two in total, twelve of whom were female and six of them in various stages of pregnancy. More importantly, he said, we hope you've enjoyed yourselves? We certainly have. He kept a quiet chuckle to himself, grinding his teeth so that his gums achieved a good rub against the lining of his inner cheeks.

As you know, we are The Boil. Myen introduced his band mates again to the room and watched as their eyes focussed on a single image of him. A silhouette of his band mates had formed in the background, hugged by tiny strays of dispersed light from a lamp that hung above. The room filled with applause a third time. Thank you, Christopher said, and followed it one last time with a weighty bow.

He heard the voice of one Fleur Dominica as clear as crystal. She cleared the phlegm in her throat and was about to say something. Bravo! she said at last. You play like gods, if the gods had learnt to play.

Chapter 4.
Drawn Sleep

Fleur…. Tamide called out. Fleur Dominica, she called out a second time in the hope she could win her back from the lethargy of a hypnotic session into consciousness. Fleur, she called a third time, who is Christopher Myen? She tapped on her shoulder. Christopher – you kept saying his name. Fleur, who is he? Tamide quizzed.

Christopher?

Yes, Fleur. Tamide Queiros was holding the base of a porcelain dish where incense burnt, exuding wild sage and roasted cedar and sending a drift of smoke towards Fleur Dominica, who was in a daze from a herbal brew.

Well, he was sitting watching the horses. I never saw horses of such magnitude before or knew they were so perceptive, but there he sat, watching the horses until dawn. He did not move until the sun came up and broke through the clouds, faint as cotton that morning. It puzzled me why he kept watching the horses, and on what seemed like a whim, he chanted the word 'solis'. I looked it up; it's another word for the sun. Solis has come out to play, he kept saying.

Solis? quizzed Tamide.

Yes, he said solis. I found it strange at the time, added Fleur, but before I could make any sense of it, it wittered away in my sleep; then I saw him again, sound asleep in his bed. I saw the thoroughbred drinking from a pool of water and in a joy dance at victory over an unknown cause. This puzzled me too.

But who is he, this Christopher Myen? asked Tamide.

Christopher? said Fleur.

Yes, this Christopher you speak of.

Then the voice of Ella Fitzgerald, said Fleur.

What about her? quizzed Tamide.

Well, she sang him a song, a song as he bathed, a song of pain, of old pain, like that of slaves. It was as though he was washing himself black and the horse's spunk would strengthen him from the inside out as he drank it.

These… dreams? quizzed Tamide.

Yes, these dreams, Fleur replied. And then boiling the horse's skin, the act of boiling it, so rich in collagen, to make strings and music like Ella Fitzgerald's before she overdosed herself on horse's glue and faded herself away into a mist.

You saw all this in your dreams? quizzed Tamide.

Yes, I did. I saw him play on a stage, his piccolo Bb, and the strain of pain that rested upon his face as he blew an embouchure like never before.

Intriguing. But who is he? You kept saying his name,

Fleur.

In a small apartment, 21B, with casings that leaked through the cracks, he told me once he saw shadows.

Shadows? quizzed Tamide.

Yes, said he saw them voyeuristically – of a woman that danced on top of him.

A woman? quizzed Queiros.

Yes, a woman. He said she whispered in the dark and quizzed him about a time long gone; she made a puzzle out of everything. And when he woke up, he noticed he'd made a mess of his bed as it smelt of pungent musk, of alkaline bleach and of magnesium and calcium salts.

A woman? quizzed Tamide.

Yes, a woman.

Intriguing, stated Tamide and made notes in her pad.

He said he thought at some point in the night they had levitated, swirling over and around his bedpost in a sun dance and that the shadows had watched with a grin, some as healthy as reverent smiles, but they couldn't have been theirs as they never mimicked them. And that's when he handled his piccolo Bb; it was as though he had suddenly come upon a poem.

He said this? quizzed Tamide.

Yes, he did.

But who is he?

A musician of some sort.

Well… you kept saying his name, over and over again.

I did?

Yes, you did. He must have meant something, at least been someone of significance? Tamide probed as she bit on the end of the plastic pen, in high hopes that all had been a casual cry from her client's subconsciousness and nothing more.

You said he played. What did he play? Quieros quizzed.

The piccolo, a bronze little number, and he was good at it; so good that he pulled me into an abyss until I fell and collapsed into him.

You collapsed into him?

Well, as in I could never look back again.

Sounds a lot like love, stated Tamide.

Well, something like it. I have known better fraudsters and tricks men than Babil.

You speak like a true poet, Fleur, but who is he, this Myen?

Christopher Myen, you ask? Well, he is blessed. I'd say blessed as much as he is cursed, and his music is only a small part of it.

You have a strange way of calling him your friend, said Tamide.

Well, he is not. The boy's made better friends out of hallucinogens, and he talks of statues with names and a Bombay that he calls Baba. I'd say these are his friends, not me.

I sense anger, Fleur. Are you angry with him? asked Tamide. Has he upset you in some way, perhaps? Perhaps all isn't as valid as you think it is? She paused to make notes.

Oh, all is valid, I can assure you, as valid as the pittas' morning calls of dependency on the daylight, stated Fleur.

So your dreams aren't drawn, drawn out of some torture so that you might want to humiliate him too? quizzed Tamide.

It can't be that simple as I also look up to him. It would have been much easier to humiliate him in person, don't you think? I'd say mine are real, as drawn as they might seem, stated Fleur.

Or perhaps it's as primal and simple as pure jealousy? prompted Quieros. Jealous of what? asked Fleur. His dreams, the woman in them? I don't suppose you think she's real, do you?

I certainly don't. It's a figment of his fragmented imagination, that's all.

Chapter 5.
Fleur Dominica's Story

Fleur Dominica recognised the themed gradient of notable topics on Psychotherapy spanned across the wood build. She allowed herself the grace of an empty whisper, subdued by the ambience of an O Kaori burning a good burn, until her eyes fell upon an over-spill of literature piled next to an occupied armchair and the swinging of a heeled shoe over a mud earth tone, that made it feel more like a room meant for a psychic read than for a medical consultation.

Tamide Quieros counted down to ten and waited for the passage of a few fleeting moments, moments for the ylang ylang, wild sage and roasted cedar to kick in. Fleur Dominica rested in a chaise longue where the leather married to her form, leaving a mould of her back. She shut her eyes in the comfort of the burn of the infused oil.

Can you tell me about your childhood? Tamide asked.

Well, nothing special; things little girls do, really.

Can you remember anything unusual?

Unusual?

Yes, unusual in your household, where you grew up?

Hmmm... I don't recollect anything being tremendously out of place. I had good parents, if that's what you're asking me; well, to my knowledge.

Okay, let's try another approach, Tamide suggested. Can you tell me when you last experienced these dreams?

Well, not precisely sure. I am not sure of the times. I know I am not being of help. But I really do want you to help me figure out these dreams, what they mean or meant at the time.

Tamide adjusted her reading glasses so the polyamide frame rested between the ridge of her lips, then she examined her patient with the scrutiny of a chef's inspection. Fleur's youth and beauty struck like a matchstick to a box as she watched her semi-clothed body adrift in a dreamlike state.

What sort of toys did you get as a little girl? asked Tamide.

Toys? Well, I got all sorts of toys as a little girl. I remember Molly, my little doll with wooden shoes; yes, I do remember her. She would crackle whenever I took her for a walk and father hated it; he hated it as he wanted to work in his study, and that's where Molly liked to go wander the most. Molly? Tamide asked.

Yes, Molly.

Was Molly the only doll you owned?

No, there were others, others but I liked Molly the most.

And why did you like Molly the most? Tamide asked.

I suppose I liked her eyes, big, pearly and coral blue. They were so pretty.

Did your other dolls have beautiful eyes? Oh yes, they did, some just as pearly and coral blue, too.

So what made Molly so special, then? asked Tamide.

Hmmm… I don't know. I'm not so sure why. I just picked her up the whole time. I liked to brush her hair; it was bright auburn.

Bright auburn you say?

Yes, bright auburn.

Tamide adjusted her position in her armchair and relaxed her projections of educated notions with the pleasure of a hunch. She replaced her reading glasses on the ridge of her nose, giving her a more acute sense of sight, and measured with clarity the naked body of Fleur Dominica resting comfortably on her chaise longue, in awe of how easily she had allowed herself to be so spirited away in only a few trying moments. Her decency extruded through the delicate fabric she had worn that day, much of which did a poor job of concealing her body. Yes, bright auburn, she'd said.

Did any of your other dolls have hair as bright as auburn? Tamide asked, carefully watching her young patient adrift in a trance.

Not that I can recall. Why do you ask? questioned Fleur.

It's just a formality. You can breathe – there is no need to tense, said Tamide.

I remember my Aunt Dupe. She, too, had bright auburn hair.

Aunty Dupe?

Yes…. My Aunt Dupe.

Your father's younger sister?

Yes, my father's younger sister.

Were you two close? asked Tamide.

Well, we were, sort of. I'd say yes and no.

What do you mean, yes and no? Tamide asked.

Well, she sort of never came around the house anymore.

Did you know why she never came around? questioned Tamide.

Well, she died before I was born. That's what my father told me; he spoke little about her.

So you say you never met her? Tamide asked.

No, not really. Not since I started to bleed.

Okay, let's try another approach, Tamide suggested. Can you tell me what you meant by this? Tamide read out a scribble from her pad: 'I have dreams about spies. I feel like I am being watched, like constantly.'

It must have been in one of my other dreams – intriguing isn't it? My other dreams, like trying on an old pair of shoes that just wouldn't quite fit, but they were mine alright, added Fleur.

Yes, intriguing. All your dreaming seems to be intriguing, stated Tamide.

But when I wake up, all seems to be normal again.

Well, that's usually what happens when we wake from

dreams, commented Tamide. Now, how about the boy, Christopher?

Christopher Myen?

Yes, Christopher Myen.

Well, what about him?

Well, I am curious. You kept saying his name, over and over again; it was quite baffling to watch. I'm so sorry, I didn't mean to spook you.

Oh, no, you didn't! You didn't spook me at all. If anything, I found it a bit revealing, as though you had some sort of connection to him.

I wish it were as simple as that. You're tired, Fleur. Now sleep, Tamide said and closed the cover of her notebook.

When Fleur Dominica woke up a second time, she witnessed a deer seated in the place of her oneirologist, Tamide Quieros. It spoke in the voice of Tamide Quieros: Like Chinese whispers, you say; that they went on for days at a time, for six moons, you say, until that very night when your ears were kissed by the grace of a different tune, Christopher Myen's, you say, and of his horn playing a piccolo brass number like you've never heard him play before. You can wake now, Fleur… Wake, Fleur Dominica heard the deer say to her

Chapter 6.
Conveyor of Cognisance

Tamide Quieros's polyamide dangled from her fingers. A blazing fight broke out between her abject reasoning and the brilliance of her comprehension; there was a toss-up between the sheet and a battle for dominance between the two constructs in her mind. She reached for sanity from the upper shelf of a wood build and puzzled over her client's higher faculty.

A tiny spec would do. Tamide Quieros yearned for lucidity, anything that could shed some light on the deliriousness of Fleur Dominica's dreams. She waved through the pages of a journal, so musk-consumed that it carried with it the brilliance of lignin and aged algae and weighed as much as lazurite. She stopped only to examine the lettering at the top of the pages and scorned the headings. She read aloud to herself in her mind, full of contempt as though the journal had failed to deliver on a distant promise. From the pages, she hoped to receive a gleam of wisdom, some inspiration to her reasoning, an insight into why she had diagnosed Dominica as mentally unstable and having taken a turn for the worst. She had written in her pad that she deemed her dispossessed of all sense of reality, cut off from the world, even in the minuteness of the details of the life she lead as a courtesan on the three nights she didn't work the tables serving up dark roast coffee of Peruvian origin. (Admittedly, it had been of a fraudulent source, and its proprietress had been too frugal to bother with its authenticity, clocking it up to her excellent negotiation skills and overlooking the obvious sheen of oil that the sacks of coffee beans gave off in the light of day. They could only have been sourced from an origin of much higher temperature and from soils so rich in nitrogen that an over-roast was needed to give them a decent shot at tasting anything like the coffee from Peru.)

Tamide Quieros deemed Fleur Dominica's dreams not as random occurrences but more as a result of possible turmoil in her past, a childhood perhaps disturbed by experiences underpinned by assault. She pressed on with the topic, drawing resolutely on her professional knowledge in the field of dream interpretation. She weighed up the transposed gestures of Fleur Dominica, from the way that she moved her head, letting it take prominence over the rest of her body, tilting it to avoid the light from the filament, then to her torso, making it move as though 60 pounds of the finest calf from the hills of Poales had been consumed by a python and the motion of the reptile was as gentle as the sea washing onto the shore at low tide, then to her valley of clove and the sweetness of imagined trickled honey she associated with it.

The smoke from the wild sage and roasted cedar filled the air with aromas of comfort. Fleur Dominica, in her most transient of exchanges, found herself in conversations of cognisance, although most of it had been lost on her with the incense already gone to her head. She resided in a place not necessarily between worlds of wonder but more with an acute sense of watery illusions, such as the Indian with a flute enticing a cobra with a tune so entrapping that the reptile buckled to the constant penetrating hums and shrills, lying lifeless and waiting for the Indian to finish him off.

Tamide Quieros placed the journal back on the shelf and fingered her way through the hardbacks, hoping for inspiration or a hint to an answer to the questions she pondered. It can't be so visceral yet so cinch, she mused.

Those ones of the snake and the snake charmer, Fleur Dominica blurted out, letting go of the quiet she'd built in her head, drenched in dimethyl-tryptamine and with the same preference for solitude as her oneirologist.

The air sped through the two reed pipes – that was the way I saw it – Fleur said, and when it hit my ears, they imploded, the Indian with the pungi and the sweet melodies that followed it. When I felt them, it was as though I had fallen into yet another one.

A dream within a dream? quizzed Tamide.

Yes, precisely. When I saw myself, I was naked as the

snake, enticing the charmer with my form, and the Indian with a semblance of my Aunt Dupe. Intriguing, murmured Tamide, without making any effort to move her pen across the pristine white paper. It's just like Paul Trouillebert's painting.

And who might that be? asked Fleur.

The French Orientalist with the famous case of a Corot forgery, the Dumas one.

When the familiarity of ink against paper returned, fleet and fierce as wild gazelles evading a pack of drooling canines, a thought lingered longer than usual with Fleur Dominica. The workings of burnt incense had consumed misgivings she'd built before she had collapsed into the leather and surrendered herself to the serenades of the incense, the herbal brew in her blood boiling away into a heist.

It's wild, she blurted out, but if snakes didn't have such a nasty bite, they did be an absolutely vulnerable thing.

Yes, snakes can be a vulnerable thing, commented Tamide, some even non-venomous, yet they manage to thrive. It's the premise of being threatened, then they strike. Did you feel threatened, Dominica? Tamide asked.

No, not particularly; more bemused, stated Fleur.

Your Aunt Dupe, did she happen to have a habit of keeping pets? questioned Tamide.

No, not that I know of. As I said, I never met her, Fleur added.

I know. It's just a formality then, Tamide scribbled.

Without care, the ink of aqueous and crystalline-dyed pigment ran a loop on Tamide's paper, the pulp soaking it up like a cub suckling on its mother's teat. The only thing visible from the inquisitive scribble was a blur of dashes and intermittent gaps that looked more like Morse code than the writing of a professional at work.

So do you think that I am losing it? asked Fleur Dominica, in high hopes she would, from Tamide Quieros, get an easy out and that the answers she had long hoped for would be at the very tips of Tamide Quieros's fingers. She wished that her punitive revelations would be her sanctuary, rescuing her from an obscurity that would have made even the most put-together of beings feel wretched.

It's your subconscious at play, Tamide Quieros stated, something buried coming to light. It's quite normal, she added.

What could it be, then, a snake and an Indian charmer? asked Fleur Dominica.

Well, for one, there is a state of unrest at play. Hence, the snake and the Indian. I suppose there could also be a good degree of deceit at play here, Tamide Quieros added and scribbled more illegible scrawl onto the page of pristine white. There could be a good degree of re-birth too, Fleur, suggested Tamide, observing the sumptuous skin on display that could only lead straight to a valley of hedonic perils, a world of feathered releases promising the reoccurrence of a state of perfect happiness. Quieros drooled a quiet release that she hid with perfect professionalism.

My Aunt Dupe? asked Fleur Dominica. Could it be that she is the deceit, the one person I hardly knew, posing as a close confidant? Fleur persisted.

Perhaps the boy, the one you kept calling Christopher Myen. Play me a tune, you said in your dreams. You mentioned he played with great talent and that he captured your soul with the subtlety of an ointment to a fly.

Fleur Dominica spirited away into the chromium of the processed leather, her skin inches from the leather's toxins and her curated disposition comfortable in its salt. Only you can know for sure, Tamide said, what's distortion and what's real. I am merely a conveyor of cognisance, she added.

But these dreams I am having – some so relevant and yet some so meaningless, Fleur Dominica sighed.

I have helped others with theirs, and I'm sure I can help you with yours, said Tamide Quieros. You'll just have to be a little bit patient. It could take a while. Now sleep, Tamide Quieros said.

Fleur Dominica woke up a third time, witnessing the faintest of possibilities that the voices she'd heard had been more of a clinical dialogue than a conversation with a counsellor, and the violent pulsation of a hydraulic pump releasing air from a compressed oxygen cylinder generated a blurry vision of a body on life support.

Keep an eye on the pulse, she heard. Below 75 and not

more, the voice gently instructed. Fleur Dominica saw that the whiteness of the room had overtaken the eclectic decor of Tamide Quieros's office. She never again saw Tamide Quieros through the veil of professionalism but rather as a friend, a companion on whom she could offload.

She heard the drips of saline drop two at a time, with a rubber's smooth accent, as the liquid travelled through her. She knew precisely when the bullet of liquid barbital entered her body, driving her into a wild spiral of a nervous goose chase dance and a do-away with distress. She was left in the dark to nurse on six ounces of idleness.

Fleur Dominica woke up a fourth time in the hours of fine grain and grass. She witnessed herself in a battle stance, although it was lost on her who it was she had confided in and who it was she had been so comfortable with, languishing on a chaise longue with the head of a deer on a human body speaking back at her.

Chapter 7.
Highspeed 42126

They dripped with the sweat that had become a companion of their hardship, and on their faces lay a cast of resilience. Their tools struck the earth and showered dirt across their backs like dissipating wings. Their measured exertions had the rhythm of drum beats, that old, traditional way of working the fields with a hoe, making ridges out of the dirt.

Further along, he noticed a stunted oak tree standing perfectly, as though painted onto the landscape by an artist. Above the tree circled a hawk, and from its beak dangled its prey, the mangled flesh twitching across the skies. As the train travelled along and approached the dark hole of the tunnel, Christopher looked back and took in one last glance of the fields. He noticed a brancher calling, the sound faint and hidden beneath the jitter of the train tracks. He took no particular note of the bird's cries but sensed the burning hunger in the throat of the young bird. Then the train disappeared into the darkness.

When Christopher Myen opened his eyes in the dark space thrust upon him by the passage of the train through the tunnel, he sensed echoes of metal grinding and the irritation of steel making metal love out of frustrated friction and sparks out of pursued leverage. None of the flickering images that appeared to him in the dark was more intriguing than that of Christina DeSilva, her hair as dark as a Friesian, so dark that even the darkness of the tunnel struggled to outdo her, pumped as if on steroids and poised as the thoroughbred that he watched chewing on the finest of alfalfa blended with barley straw infused with oil. She was sitting idly looking back at him in the vacancies of what seemed like spirit deficit. It was as though she had been sitting there the whole time, opposing him like mist to boiling water. It took but a few trying moments, she said and spirited away like a bleep.

Christopher Myen woke a second time and allowed the workings of a lump down his throat. The running pace of a quickset hedge caught his gaze as the train sped along the track. He allowed his head to rest upon the upholstery and took a deep breath of the air plummeting down from the propelling fan hanging from the coach's ceiling. It circulated at a steady pace barely audible to his ears. *42126*. There, in all their splendour, etched into the silver plaque above the entrance to the cabin, he instantly recognised them.

Christopher Myen's eyes settled on the numbers like a heap of debris from a fall, a numeronym that hung delicately among the dark slumbered visions of his mind. He sat motionless, picking up the gentle wind drifting in through the slit of the window. The hazel bushes ran alongside the tracks, wild as the day they had been grown, brilliantly demarcating where the open fields started and where the train company owned the lands.

The image of Christina DeSilva ran rounds of kaleidoscope in his head. Then it diffused into liquid drops of syrup, and the taste of sugar left his tongue numb. He sensed the same scent of old rose in a vase of aged lavender water and recollected moments around his bed, the floating shadows, the ones that never mimicked them, and the porcelain that moved in unison, giving quiet remakes of smirks as they counted scores and watched Christina dance above his torso.

Christopher argued that he had, in fact, been duped into these visions. He disputed the thrills as illusions of hallucinogens, clever tricks played by his own mind to fool him, perhaps self-preservation from imminent so-called danger. She seems to assume she knows me, he thought, as if we've met before, some place, some time. It's all just a trick, some foolery, he disputed and collapsed into the upholstery.

So did you miss me? he heard the voice of Christina DeSilva ask. You left, she said. You never thought to say goodbye, she added. I woke up like a light, and like a light you were gone. Remember the aviary? she prompted, still very much in a state of anxious paralysis.

The two pittas! The two that chirped all through the warm summer nights? 'Yellow, yellow!' she whispered. Mustard yellow, just like the brush strokes. You do remember the brush strokes? Your brush strokes, she added. You were quite good at them.

The last time I lifted a paint brush I was twelve, with all the worrying tendencies of an adolescent boy and the pining for the attention of a nescient young girl, he thought but kept it to himself.

The old shaman, the warehouse – do you remember? she went on.

He felt his tongue heavy and his ears struggling to place where the voice had come from – everywhere. It seemed to him that it had sieved in through the walls and the panels and the ceiling where the fan pulsed steadily and the seats empty of occupants into the atmosphere where it gathered like a storm, sifting through the air like a poisonous leak from a burst pipe.

The faint sounds of wind continued to crash upon the window pane; the panel carried on rattling for something like an hour. Christopher Myen opened his eyes and saw himself seated in a coach numbered 3-TC-42126-LKA. It wasn't a dream after all, Christopher Myen thought. This rain is real; it's pouring out there. I can hear it. When his breathing grew heavy again, he fell into yet another dream and saw the golden shimmer of his piccolo Bb trumpet reaching him deep in his sleep. He recollected moments he'd last played, seeing himself up on a stage depressing the small pistons on his trumpet. With both the anguish and delight of an alluring Indian sultana, he witnessed the play of music in the air, marvelling that the sounds of his own trumpet had induced an audience to deliquesce.

You never seem to wonder anymore, Christopher? he heard Christina say to him. You've lost your wonder – that part of you at least, she added. You've let your curiosity get away from you; you've replaced it with stone. You ever wonder how it is we always seem to meet like this? she quizzed.

As the old train sped on, a whole day seem to pass him by in which he had little comprehension of the phantom hanging from his reasoning except for the gentle clues she left, studious as flashcards for an approaching exam. High in the skies, the sun burned an intense glow of orange, a richness of wild auburn laced in the clouds that marked the start of a crisp summer evening. Christopher allowed himself to be spirited away yet again. He took in the redness of the ripples that married the clouds to the skies and contemplated which had been more charming, the farmlands he'd seen in the morning or the skies of the evening where the sun-burnt hydrogen and helium formed the backdrop to speed highway 42126 shrinking into the distance.

Chapter 8.

Deep

The quiet – it's like an old friend lingering in the dark; it's there when you're all alone, deserted and abandoned; it cosies up to you like in cold winters when all is gone and at night times when all is asleep. Do you remember? Christopher heard the voice of Christina DeSilva basking beneath multitudes of tiny shiny lights. We counted them once, one by one, she said. We did those shiny things, do you remember? We ran our thumbs over and over, as far as the wandering star Janus, deep blue as the ocean, and we were close, so close we made maps and tracks out of them from one twinkle to the next, do you remember? Until we could no longer keep count, she added.

My eyes are heavy; are yours? They're heavy, as they always seem to be. I knew, the moment I set eyes on you, you would be mine; finally, you came back to me, Christopher heard DeSilva whisper. He realised that it could all be only in a dream and that everything was pretty much not happening to him but rather from him. Christopher felt the warmth of DeSilva's breath, reticent as the embrace of lost love and the pining for sugar. Her lungs expanded into a balloon of admired desires, and their collapse was like the tragedy from a bullet, ablaze like wild fire in the moments of extreme euphoria until the clock struck midnight.

I lost you once. Christopher heard the almost narcoleptic instincts of fallen love and struggled to pull himself out of a waking dream. He walked through the corridor of Christina DeSilva's persuasion to the next instance of her childlike innocence. The smell of salts, a yearning for clarity and the pinch of cold dropped onto his chest. DeSilva's inquisition had turned into a burst of murmurs. I am reaching for myself, she said. When I wake, I realise I did been in yet another dream and am still very much asleep. Christopher woke to find himself seated with the same degree of tranquillity as the Bombay in the late afternoon.

The two pittas with mustard bellies danced about their little territory. Fresh foliage from the green landscape made its way up his nose, as easy as Sunday afternoons. Christopher recognised the hard top and the stone pavement that led to nowhere in particular but a wavering image of himself that he coined Isomer me.

Isomer me, he heard himself say, we are a good ten years apart, and yet you've managed to outdo me. You've grown into a proficient sense of myself like a shadow of atonement. Where I've failed, you've excelled, and where I've stalled, you've proceeded with grace like a twin cut from a coat tail with wisdom to hand. This image of Christopher Myen looked unlike an image in a mirror but rather like himself ten years in the making, with all the flaws he conceded to from his late adolescence to early adulthood laced around his torso like charms from an Inca. His face had become that of a man who resembled himself, although rather astute in the rituals of daily uncertainties and far from being done with his unusual manner of staring into the abyss in the early mornings, waiting on a muse, languishing on Tenet literature, even though none had given him an insight into a way of living with his vices. When he played, he allowed himself to be influenced by the draws of amphetamine, seeing his music blossom through a hallowed lens of hallucinogens.

On the stage, the light was dim and the room was empty of an audience. The air thinned like a slice of ice on freshwater solidifying from an impurity. He witnessed the richness of the timbre of the slow playing of his piccolo Bb, like gently walking on water. Listening to his music filled his head with imaginations of flight. At a point, his band mates joined in, adding to the marvellous music fantasia. The gran cassa that Ayer Frederickson played created gentle rattles that were somewhat more mathematical than emotional. When his mallet went against the mylar, it was about war and peace, adding two degrees of heat to the room and keeping the time. When he swapped it for the rute made of bamboo sticks, it evoked something very Jewish from within him, like lighting a candle on Hanukkah, although he hadn't practised the faith or believed in any of its values. It was more a secular inheritance, beating on the rims of the drum kit with the rute of bamboo sticks. They, of course, made vibrations that sounded more like a whispering chant than a dusty thrashing on metal, like the Greek god Apollo. Chiyoko Matsukawa, who was also in Christopher's band, allowed the moving images to elude him, playing his gold and white piano to reduce the chaos of Ayer Frederickson's drumming. When Ayer thundered on the drum kit, Chiyoko's easy playing cooled it down like a damp cloth. Eventually, he grew selfish and played into a drift of dreamy melodies. He found himself standing idly at the Shinkansen station in Tokyo, with the single thought of his father's well-being weighing on his shoulders like a brick on a pile of paper in a gust of wind. These images were as vivid to Chiyoko Matsukawa now as they were when he was twelve; he saw the sternness on the faces of men drawn from one of Tokyo's most dangerous Hontoni and the threat of murder from a blade of a katana. When he returned to his Steinway, it was with the heavy temptation to fleet with yet another solo, this time Ludwig van Beethoven's Moonlight Sonata, third movement, even though he hadn't been in an orchestra but rather in Christopher Myen's cool jazz band. Against Chiyoko's troublesome playing, Christopher Myen could only see Sebastian Evans as a scaffold, a much-needed piece of staging to stabilise their music. He played the double bass and kept the time, playing a scale that he pretty much stuck to for the duration of their playing, the same 2-5-1, until Christopher awoke to the realities of daytime.

Chapter 9.
In a Day

According to the daily ritual of Christopher Myen, he first removed the crust from his eyes, rubbing away the remnant of sleep that remained in them. He cleared his head of drowsy beliefs with a great yawn and motioned himself out of bed, walking towards the small bathroom cluttered with unkempt toiletries and laundry that could have been done weeks before, although it looked as though it had been left in a basket for some other task. Christopher relished his sleep and hated early mornings. In front of the mirror, he picked out his blue toothbrush and applied paste from a tube that lay uncapped. He gave himself an indifferent look as if the day ahead was predetermined and he knew what was going to happen every single moment. When he finished brushing his teeth and was satisfied with their cleanliness, he paid attention to his face, observing his eyes and how dull they had become, as though emptied of life. It seemed he was merely existing, just meant to be breathing but with no innate purpose. Then he thought of his dreams from the night before and knew they were unlike his other dreams.

He stood listening to the rush of water from the tap, and for a moment this satisfied him. He waited a while and then collected some of it in his palms and applied it to his face. When the coldness had washed away the sleep, he examined his physique and the firmness of his muscles. He calculated in his head the hours of repetition and days of recovery, focusing on the strain in his muscles near his neck, and gave himself a stretch in the mirror; he then turned his attention to the other side and gave that a good stretch too. When he was finished and satisfied with the degree of relief, he had a go at his arms and gave them a good stretch, certain that whatever amount of sleep was left in his body was just about depreciated.

There, in his small bathroom, dampening his skin with a towel, he contemplated his options for breakfast, his choice of clothing and his long walk to the stop where he would board a bus that would take him to work and his daily routine of soldering copper with a plasma torch and tuning TV sets. Then he walked out of his bathroom, leaving it full of mist as though the late autumn had visited and left as soon as he had opened the door for it to escape.

For breakfast, he fixed himself some scrambled eggs and toast with chives that danced delicately on the viscous mush. To wash it back, he made a decent brew of French pressed coffee and watched the dark liquid seep to the top through the wire filter. He was certain a gulp of it would awaken a sense of purpose within him and that he would then be able to embark on his tasks for the day. He switched on the black and white TV set sitting comfortably in the corner of the room. This room was quite a bit larger than where he slept and had two large windows. Outside, a ginkgo tree provided privacy and a home for two pitta birds. He flipped through the channels, stopping only to observe the news of a hurricane in a state 200 kilometres from his home. The hurricane had been given the name Ayah. He made a quick measurement in his head and thought only of the sound of the wind and the thunder.

On a cream sofa, a Bombay cat lay unconcerned with the worries of everyday life. It watched with a certain curiosity the recently acquired meticulous movement of its owner, from the way he lifted his mug and took gentle sips to the way his eyes fixated on the set, watching the anchor's delivery of gruesome, bite-sized accounts of the hurricane's atrocities. The anchor detailed the wind speed in miles per hour and central pressure in millibars; in conclusion, the anchor announced that the hurricane would be surging for days, with estimated damage verging on the extreme. Christopher thought of it as a bull's charge directly towards a matador, who carelessly places his muleta in front of his body. The Bombay seemed to be concerned only with watching its owner shift his balance. Its faint emerald eyes moved quickly, observing and reassessing like a chef at work, only it carried out its duties with its head on the sofa and its feet in the air, exposing its penis to the heavens. When Christopher finished with the residue of fine Peruvian coffee, he walked towards the Bombay, but before he could reach to give the cat a rub on its head, it fled, escaping through the window and looking back at Christopher with more disdain than endearment, as though his attention would be much better placed on the perils of an approaching storm, even though the cat wasn't a fortune-teller or gifted in the act of psychic precognition.

Christopher walked towards the window with his piccolo Bb in his hands. He studied the mouthpiece and then gazed thoughtfully into the far shrub where the Bombay had taken refuge, staring back at him as though bewildered by the prospect of his approach. When Christopher was satisfied with the notion in his head, he blew a steady embouchure, lifting his trumpet high into the air and allowing its sounds to travel like sketches for a schematic drawing, each breath depicting the overcoming of something. At the end of his playing, he put down his trumpet, put on his shoes and exited the room.

Chapter 10.
Outside

Outside, the air was crisper than usual and thinner than a sheet of banana paper. Christopher's first coherent observation was the brilliance of the green in every single thing that lived an immobile existence. After he had become comfortable with the impression of the vegetation, he took a deep breath that filled his nasal passages with an extremely alkaline smell. He was certain it was horse dung from the way the quality malt and barley lingered long in the air. After the stench had dissipated, he focused his attention on the irregularity of his shirt, adjusting it so it sat comfortably on his shoulders, and gave his shoes a quick inspection, as though half the world wasn't falling apart 200 kilometres away from where he stood. Once satisfied with the tidiness of his sneakers, he glanced at the Bombay and saw that it was still sitting beneath the fuchsia denticulata, licking its paws and cleaning its face.

Christopher allowed the notion of letting sleeping dogs lie to rest upon his consciousness, although, in the case of the feline, he was wise to its propensity for mischief, such as bringing garden mice into his apartment to toy with them under the evening moon in summer or chasing pigeons up trees, killing them at the slightest opportunity and displaying their dead bodies on his floor like trophies from a sport while making pitiful meows for attention.

On this occasion, however, the Bombay became quickly satisfied with a dose of external validation and did not need to meet Christopher's gaze, instead focusing its attention on the pittas nestled above in the ginkgo tree and drowning itself in the drug of their music.

Being careful not to miss out on his calling for the day or to be stood up by destiny, Christopher took carefree steps along the pavement, mimicking the wind that blew through the cotton of his hair. He passed by the shop owned by a merchant of the orient who had none of the qualifying attributes of an Asian except for his pudginess in middle age and his increasingly developing dislike for blacks or any semblance of a mulatto. It would be threatening for him to imagine a world where the blacks weren't a victim of societal objection. On this occasion, however, the slight sight of Christopher had prompted him to hurry out of his store, without even locking his cash register, and make his way to the pavement. He wished Christopher a good day and good fortune, expressing the hope that all would be well with him and, even more, that all he ever experienced in life would be to his liking.

Christopher mistook the Oriental's civility for a ploy as it had been too out of character for a man who considered that profits were much more valuable than any measure of morality, although, on this occasion, it seemed genuine and lacked any of the usual cunning housed in his motives. Christopher went about his day, paying little attention to the man but simply acknowledging him with a nod and a smile. The shop owner's name was Mr Yamamoto Kasuga.

On his route was the cafe serving nothing but the best of supposedly Peruvian coffee. Its proprietress had readily allowed herself to be conned into purchasing the roasted coffee beans for a fraction of their usual cost, assured of the vast margins to be made compared to her usual takings. On this occasion, however, she was in a spat about how the coffee beans hadn't lived up to her expectations, although it had taken her over 23 months to become aware of their flaws or to raise any concerns over their shortcomings. It had simply been too convenient for her to pass the bags up as authentic and to play on the intelligence of both her employees and patrons.

When Christopher reached the shop front, he saw the dreamy Fleur Dominica waiting on tables. She didn't notice him standing there for nearly a minute, and when she finally chanced to notice his presence, she seemed not to recognise him. Christopher was sure it was her he had been playing solo to in the vacant downtown hall where the light had been so low it was as though he was playing to a shadow. Her hair was the colour of fire, like an alatus plant, and her demeanour was more serene than her outward appearance.

Christopher made a mental note of these contrasting realities, and when he walked past the railway station, it looked as if it had been abandoned for something like a decade, which puzzled him. According to his recollection, it had been only yesterday he'd boarded the train to Yeovil, a town 20km south of his hometown, where he would meet with his band mates and practice their free jazz until the moon started to show its face. When he reached the bus terminal, he was relieved that this one location was the same as he remembered it. He bought his ticket from the vendor sitting behind a shield of glass and made his way to his point of boarding. He made another mental note that the vendor had an unusual pattern of hair growth, undecidedly bald, and wore on his chin a beard of ginger. What puzzled him the most was when the bus finally arrived at its post to pick up its passengers, it seemed that the same undecidedly bald man who had sold him the ticket was now driving the bus, unless he had a twin and both worked for the bus company. Christopher boarded the bus, showing his ticket so it could receive the customary puncture, and sat in the middle of the bus next to a window, resigning himself to watching the world go by.

Chapter 11.
The Journey Out

It took a little while for Christopher to notice the gypsy on the bus. Her fragrance was of walnut and mandarin, with subtle hints of ocean salt, and she wore her clothing of dark, earthy fabric with consummate ease. Each layer was somewhat different in style, yet they all matched. It was difficult to tell whether she was present in person or merely in spirit, whether she was indeed sitting at the back of the bus or was merely a lingering ghost that haunted the poor souls of commuters on board bus 42126.

Christopher settled himself into the upholstery of foam and matelasse and drifted into sleep. When he awoke, he found himself in the company of strangers and drifters. He observed the escaping sun tuck itself behind a cloud of silver-grey that seemed more like a monument to misery than a natural weather change. After a short while, all the drifters and travellers were seated at something akin to a restaurant, with a rubber canopy for roofing. In the face of the impending storm, conversation turned to the hurricane, appropriately named Ayah, and its potential for destruction. A moment later, the rain began to pour down, and half a dozen frozen fish fell from the sky, piercing the canopy and startling the occupants, who had been waiting for a waiter. A few moments passed before another dozen frozen fish fell from the sky and again struck the rubber canopy. They were the colour of a northern red snapper but had pointy, razor-sharp mouths that penetrated the rubber, leaving half their faces and their bodies sticking out into the air.

This puzzled the occupants of this kind of restaurant on flat terrain at a high altitude. They were gathered in some place reminiscent of the Himalayas as the temperature was similar, and, in Christopher's estimation, it had the same humidity many had spoken about and associated with the Himalayan north. When the cloud finally grew weak and gave in to a storm of biblical proportions, it was with the fall of northern-looking frozen red snappers that quickly covered the ground. After a short while, other exotic fish species fell to the ground, except these were fresh out of the sea, rather than frozen. It seemed as though the whole world had turned on its head and emptied the sea of its aquarian life. When the storm had passed and the expectancy of human nature took its toll, Christopher and his fellow drifters gathered up the snappers in sacks, filled to the brim, until they could not fit any more in and had them bursting from the mouth of the sacks. Then new characters arrived on the scene and walked past the restaurant with the most exquisite sea crustaceans, from wild shrimps to sea crabs and the very best of lobsters. They soon became the envy of the drifters and travellers, who had received only the frozen red snappers and a few exotic fish.

This dream of Christopher's faded away, and when he awoke, he found himself at some kind of a gala, with the likeness of one Christina DeSilva standing by his side like a bride or lover of some sort. She was wearing the most exquisite ballgown made of crystals and silver silk and looked as though all the stars of the skies had cumulated with her and, in their conspiracy, she had come to be by his side.

It's good to see you again, she said, and if you don't mind, I would like to excuse myself. She made her way to a spiral staircase and disappeared through one of the many archways that led to the living quarters. The party itself seemed more of a cerebral occasion, of no specific purpose than to indulge in the very best of wines and relish the opulence of the occasion itself. Christopher didn't recognise any of the guests except for Christina DeSilva. When she reappeared, it wasn't to be by his side but in the midst of the crowd, like a jewel, and in his line of sight, watching a contortionist put on a show for the audience. He responded to instant intuition and approached her, planting a kiss on her back beneath her exposed shoulder. She turned around and said to him in her most commending voice, now this time you have done it right.

When Christopher awoke, he found himself in the company of the gypsy sitting on the opposite side, with a resolute look on her face. Her eyes were covered by the darkest of sunshades and she wore a smirk that said more about her innate sense of knowing and reading the course of the future than it did to invite small talk. She sat as though waiting for a conversation and eventually took it upon herself, summoning up a courage that could have been gained only from her years of maturity. It is good to see you again, she said finally.

Chapter 12.
Deep Phase of the Abyss

The sounds of a trumpet playing came to Christopher's ears the way they used to do in the early hours of the morning when the surge of inspiration was raw and he could taste the elements on his tongue. He allowed the easy melody to welcome him to a place where his head was like a feather and enjoyed the euphoria that usually came with a sudden burst of inspiration. He hadn't acknowledged the presence of the gypsy or that the air had started to become something of a slice of calamity and reduced in temperature or that the sweat on his head had dissipated. In its place was a current of fresh air that could only have come from the Gulf of Past Time coast where life was slow and the humidity was like a companion of heavy conversations about religion and politics.

There is going to be a storm, the gypsy said, a very big one. They are calling it by the intentional name of Ayah. I for one can't imagine a more fitting name for a storm of this magnitude. And where is it you're headed to on a day like this?

Her name was Dupe Felicity. She had the look of an accomplished woman, in her youth a brilliant intellect, the type to relish perils and thirst after debate. She seemed to be about seventy, although it was difficult to say which side of the ripe age of seventy she was on. It was also difficult to say whether she was blind or just fancied the notion of being a mystic. After all, her vocation commanded the idea of mystery, and she hid her eyes behind sunglasses large enough to cover three-quarters of her face.

The bus travelled its normal route, making its scheduled stops. It hadn't picked up any new passengers, and the only occupants were the gypsy and the characters in the daydreams of Christopher Myen.

The driver himself looked unconcerned by the irregularities of this particular day and went about his normal duties, even though no new commuters had boarded his bus at the stops and none of its passengers had pressed the bell that indicated their stop was next. Usually, this particular route would have taken a little over an hour, giving Christopher time to get to the door of the shop where he worked, repairing TV sets and giving them a new lease of life, tuning their antenna so they could receive the little waves of the analogue signal that was accessible to the region. The hurricane had been on Christopher's mind. He pondered its magnitude and the destruction likely to follow in its path. He thought if anyone were to survive its possible impact on the town of Lunaceworth, it would be the Bombay, Kamari, by its nature bouncing back from any injury it acquired and its countless near misses with death.

The gypsy, Dupe Felicity, started her enquiry with a complex question. It came from a place of motherly concern. She asked about his worries and whether news of the hurricane had been weighing on his mind, but most of all, she drew his attention to her knowledge of his deep-seated desires and the dreams of the woman that recurred in the depth of the night.

Young-faced man, she said, what worries you? You will ruin that brilliant face of yours and turn it into an over-ripe peach, the gypsy said, and if you carry on, you'll end up with a cabbage for a face. What worries you, young man? she persisted, and settled on the notion of letting the birds fly in his head for an answer.

Well, you need not worry so much. All that means well ends well, she said. It's the usual way of the world. According to the gypsy, no such evil could ever exist without a good place to start. No one human is ultimately evil, and evil in essence could only ever exist in the presence of good. It's simply symbiotic: one needs the other to thrive, said the gypsy.

What do I owe her, exactly? Christopher asked as he observed her tapping on the floor of the bus with her umbrella and made out her distance from his seat in a few brief seconds.

There you are, she said. Good. You must owe her something, or she wouldn't go to so much trouble. She bothers you in the depth of night and releases the fever of lust you experience. My advice to you, beautiful-faced man, is do not fight it.

The bus came to a stop at the ultimate ringing of the bell. The gypsy rose to her feet gently as seedlings do at dawn. She wished Christopher Myen a good day and that good fortune would be his portion, assuring him that for the most part, love is a business of rejection. She navigated her way to the doors opened to the elements and with three strikes of her caned umbrella made her exit.

Christopher watched both the door of the bus and his emerging enquires close. As the ginger-bearded driver pulled away, the diminishing figure of the gypsy standing at the side of the road was like a mirage.

Chapter 13.

Man in the hallway

Minutes passed before Christopher noticed that a man had been standing in the hallway of the bus. He had watched the journey of Christopher Myen pick up confused trends and felt a quiet satisfaction that the world was exactly as it needed to be, full of disagreement and confusion, for without their existence, it would be a soulless experience and out of control.

The man had the convenience of being called the Old Major for his short spell in the Queen's army where he'd fought in the war of 1914. He also controlled the ticketing for both bus and train company and had a reputation for being a notorious autocrat. He handled all aspects of tourism for the town of Lunaceworth, from its transportation network to the pleasant green spaces, including the minute details of comfort and hospitality experienced at four of the five cafeterias in town. Each paid him a percentage of their custom. He even managed to exert his authority at three of the finest art galleries in town where a fraction of their revenue was paid to him in dividends every fourth quarter of the year.

The Old Major had the inconvenience of being built as

horizontal as humanly possible. He stood non-moving as a pole, with the shift of his eyes observing newly boarded passengers. He lacked all empathy with them and looked as though all of his winter days had come at once. His grey face was sunken and sombre, resembling a cloud canopy in a harsh and insolent season.

The hollow beneath the bridge swallowed the bus and created a dusky vacuum that rested heavily on Christopher's chest. He was certain that his journey was coming to an end and it would take only a few minutes to get to his stop where the TV repair shop was located. He adjusted himself in his seat and unwound after the bewilderment of the gypsy's sayings and the forecast of the hurricane.

Commanding attention in the usual way of the Old Major, he walked the hallway of the bus with his shoulders pinned back, focussing on a distant Christopher Myen. Ticket please, the Old Major asked. May I see your ticket?

The image of the gypsy standing at her stop and diminishing in the distance pressed on him like the memory of war-time captives. The Old Major's puncher went down and left two small holes in his ticket. The conductor smiled for the first time, his sunken eyes taking on a look of familiarity. You have a safe trip, said the Old Major.

When the Old Major was done, he walked over to the other passengers, inspecting tickets and carefully examining serial numbers, each one registered to the bus company, Midways, with the Batch Ticket Number MC398-0DB-913-42126-ZX. The last few numbers were missing from Christopher's ticket.

As the bus gathered momentum, it took a bend and straightened out onto a single lane. The driver pounded its gears, causing the bus to accelerate and producing a sensation of flight. Its occupants were sucked into their seats, and Christopher imagined clouds floating by. He witnessed himself amongst a flock of birds, swallowed into a jet stream. I am flying! he thought to himself. I am up here with the birds! Twelve swallows migrating from the harsh winter flew effortlessly into a V formation.

You seem pretty lost and falling, rather than flying, Christopher heard a voice say. You ought to focus on your strokes. It should come naturally to you, as natural as the sun's grin in the daytime and the moon's sulk at night time, but you seem to be falling into the blue sea below.

I have never flown before, not once in my life, he said, and I find this experience to be quite nauseating, with my feet off the ground and my body high in the clouds.

He found he was in a conversation with a swallow, the bird that lagged at the tail end of the V formation. It is you that sees yourself as falling; others think that you are flying and doing much better than they are, said the swallow. Spread your wings wide and relax; the rest will take its course. The others are waiting. We will lose them to the jet stream and soon all will be gone for good.

Christopher surrendered himself to the idea that even if he were to fall to earth, at least it was only in his dream; he could not have really been in conversation with a real live swallow as he hadn't known of one that could actually talk, although he couldn't fully explain to himself how all existence seemed so real to him at that moment in the skies.

I am doing it! Christopher blurted out, flapping with all his might. See – I am doing it! The soaring swallow took to the jet stream as effortlessly as the flow of water in a brook. Then Christopher looked around and found nothing but an empty cloud and around him a hoard of strange faces calling out to him. Christopher! Christopher! he heard. Christopher, wake up!

Chapter 14.
Flight 42126

In two words, Christopher could describe the notion of flight, and in eight he could describe the essence of freedom and what it meant to fly. He saw himself walking the rooms of his loft apartment 21B, shifting through the shadows of his bedroom under the watchful eye of the Bombay. He made his way to his washroom where a depleted mercury mirror showed a depiction of himself at the tender age of ten.

To the jazz in his head, a drum marked patterns of diction, keeping the beat as if the life of their music depended on it. When he finally heard his piccolo Bb, it was with a certain call from afar of a purpose unattained. It was as though there was yet much for him to achieve. The blaring trumpet carried on late into the night, with just the drumming from a distance to accompany it; he knew it could only be Ayer Frederickson's drumming.

Ayer, is it you? Christopher called out to a distant drummer hugged into the dusk. I imagine it can only be you by the way you're drumming. Would you be so kind as to help me out of these sleepless interludes as I can't seem to get myself out of them? I feel adrift, as if I am under the influence of some amphetamine, and the moon hasn't looked so good in a long time.

The drummer was consumed by his admission that nothing else existed outside of his own drumming; when he finally stopped, it was only to say that nothing really existed outside of one's own self and that everything existed on the inside. You go away in search of something, only to learn how to exist on the inside, added a serene Frederickson.

Christopher managed to engage with the furloughed Ayer Frederickson, seated on his drummer's stool with his sticks crossed waiting on a command. Everyone seems to be talking about you, Ayer said, and how you haven't been good enough and how much of a fool you've been to allow yourself to be swayed by the lure of a ghost.

And when the fever of vivacious drumming returned, it was to detach him from all reality. Ayer! Christopher called out, but he was long gone under the spell of his own drumming, beating his sticks on the mylar of his gran cassa until he reached a state of euphoria. He stopped a second time only in recognition of the fact that the moon had started to drift into its daily pilgrimage around the globe, tucking itself behind a cluster of clouds and giving them an incandescent glow. He counted with precision in his head twenty-seven-and-a-third plus another twenty-seven then began to speak.

You know, I saw your body. You were in a pretty bad

shape. It baffles me how well you've managed to get it together, and without a single hint, added a composed Frederickson. In any case, you seem to be pretty good at it. And how much amphetamine do you reckon you took?

As much as two doses and a third, replied Christopher. I can't have taken any more than that – two doses and a third.

How well can you play? I mean, if you held your piccolo this very moment, how well could you play? How well could you make that metal sing? asked Ayer.

I guess as good as any day. You've heard me at my worst; would you say this was one of them?

It makes no difference to me; I am only an illusion, said Frederickson.

So what have you done with the realness of Ayer Frederickson? What've you done with the brilliant Frederickson? asked a dazed Christopher.

Two doses and a third, you say. Only two-and-a-third, said Frederickson, yet you managed to make a fool of yourself.

If only puppets could talk! I am so confused about what's real and what's bleeding. It could only be a dream, Christopher thought to himself and called out for Frederickson.

Ayer Frederickson, he called out a second time, you seem to have taken flight and abandoned me for good. My legs are shaky bent and I can't seem to walk. Do you mind giving me a hand? he called out a third time, but the drummer had already dissipated and left behind something of a mist and a still shadow.

He later heard the voice of Frederickson say to him in the quietness of dusk, it's what the greats do. They take flight from within.

Ayer, is it you? Christopher called out a fourth time. And how do you measure two doses and a third of an amphetamine when I've only taken one? he asked in the hope of engaging the shadow.

Only one, you say? One of the cherry red pills? And why are your floors so shaky jittery? It must have been the building! It must be the forerunner of the hurricane, said the shadow.

You've heard the news, Christopher said. They are forecasting one of the worst. It was right there on TV. They are saying it's going to be a really bad one; they are calling it Hurricane Ayah, can you believe it?

Ayah, you say?

Yes, Ayah, replied Christopher. It sounds like a bad shake, if you ask me.

A bad shake and yet you have your conversations with a smoke and a shadow? Perhaps it isn't as bad as you think it's going to be.

Chapter 15.

The Forecast

The dance of pixels on a concave screen went on for hours on end, the black and the white and the grey, a notion of detachment as the continuum of crisping white noise echoed through the room. The vibration of electrical pulses resonated with every object in the room. The dial was tuned to a channel and he waited for a picture to appear. All seemed to be gone; he was aware of freedom and aware its cousin, an overbearing urge for attachment to everything humanly desirable, and he realised that his vices had been near-crippling.

When the set finally came on, it was with the ongoing presentation of the weather, with the anchor calling out points on a regional map. We should expect to see winds of 130 miles per hour north of Yeovil, the anchor said, wearing a business suit made out of a Peruvian poncho and looking more like a man who ploughed the fields for artichokes than a weather man. It would normally have made it difficult for him to look serious, but at this moment, it mattered little as there was a great storm coming and, according to the poncho anchor, hurricanes to follow in its path.

We should expect much slower winds south of Yeovil, he said, with wind speeds of about 95 miles per hour. Such a vast contrast 200 kilometres west of Yeovil, he said, raising a wooden pointer to a chart hanging behind him, depicting five great wind swirls dancing about Yeovil. We would be lucky to experience wind speeds of 98 miles per hour, said the anchor. Not a good place to be caught outside. Better to be safe than sorry, he added.

Now, south-west of Yeovil, a sparsely populated area seems to be a bit of a lucky dip and can expect wind drifts in this region with speeds of about 75 miles per hour. Still, not a safe place to be outside, although there'll be less impact from its movement than from the four other wind swirls in the region, he added. North east of Yeovil should expect speeds of about 110 miles per hour, a category 2. Later on, as the hurricane drifts offshore in somewhat of a rage, we should expect a great turbulence as it creates an energy cyclone proceeding offshore. We can expect greater speeds off the Gulf Coast, although we would have had the worst of it by then. Yes, it is going to be a bad one, the anchor said, responding to a caller on his earpiece.

Yes, that's bad, I'd say. I'd say it's on a scale we've never seen before. I'd say wind speeds could be well over 180 miles per hour, a category 6 if we've ever had one before.

Yes, I don't ever recall a category 6, said the anchor.

I guess it's a lot Ayah, higher? asked the caller.

Yes, Ayah, the anchor responded. They are calling it Ayah.

His mother-tongue Spanish crashed out of suppression. Ayah, he said. Our only saving grace is this wind is offshore, far away from land.

Christopher looked at the display of the Saffir-Simpson scale at the bottom of the screen. It occurred to him that the winds would fluctuate greatly about the region of Yeovil. It also surprised him how much the wind speed would vary 200 kilometres in every direction from the town of Yeovil. Lunaceworth was south of the region and looked a somewhat safer zone, if there was one. He made a note of the hurricane's inland speed of 130 miles per hour. That's a good category 4, then 95 miles per hour south, a category 1, he noted. 98 miles per hour west of Yeovil, a category 2, 75 miles per hour south west, well, that's not too far from here, and north east the wind speed will be110 miles per hour, a good category 2. He aligned the numbers in a series so it read 4, 2, 1, 2, with the final addition of the unclaimed offshore speeds of 180 miles per hour, a good category 6 if there was such a thing, he noted.

Christopher carried on with the business of being human. You cannot let your fears govern your thoughts, he thought. You can't not sleep for fear that the world will forget about you when you wake, he thought; the world wouldn't care, regardless. The analogue of plugs and sockets came to him in his sleep, the idea that any plug could fit into any socket of its region; they could make electricity, they could even make a spark, but it doesn't necessarily mean they couldn't short circuit into a fire.

Burn, baby, burn, he thought. The poncho anchor came back on screen, calling out points on the weather until the screen disappeared into a zip. Christopher took out a soldering wire and applied a hot touch to its end until it began to burn. He interwove two wires and began to weld until they became a solid silver. This was the repair shop where Christopher worked part time and considered a place of solace; he dedicated himself to the tuning of the TV set so they could pick up the scarce aerial signal.

By his calculation, it had been two whole days and an evening since he last played as he measured his days by his yearning for creativity; any more than two days threw him into a deep mood. He dealt with his anxiety mostly by kissing the brass metal of his trumpet, and when he couldn't, he fell into a deep state, realising that he must have lived a total of 1000 years of 12 cumulative lifetimes by his estimate.

Chapter 16.
Hurricane

In the hurricane, Christopher saw the face of DeSilva. He saw her at her most pure. He saw her as he had always done, not knowing who she really was or why she had come to him. The liquid noise of his trumpet blared and reached him deep in his sleep so that the only thing that remained with him was her surreptitious way of trying to bring out the devil in him. I was reaching – I couldn't contain myself, he said. She had the better of me.

And why is it you've been so resentful if she is but a hurricane? It baffles me how little you seem to know and how much you put at stake. You take for granted something as sacred as a hurricane? If only you knew her significance! You talk about the hurricane and her magnitude. If only you knew how grand her powers could be, but you brush it away as a mere occurrence. Only a hurricane, you say? I'd say you've underestimated her powers. You say she arouses you in the dark and comes to you at your most serene. And why do you think that is? Why do you think she seems to bothers you?

I ask that myself. I acknowledge how lucky I must have

been.

Lucky? You flatter yourself so much, Christopher. The lady comes to us all, Fleur Dominica said. My oneirologist awaits me.

She stood from her chair, adjusted the hem of her garment, turned her back to the bed and without saying another word dissipated into a mist.

The TV signal broke up, and a competent Christopher got out of bed, pulled on two wires and soldered them. Then he picked up the multimeter to check that the current was coming through. He felt a hand on his wrist and the pressure of two thumbs pushing against his artery: the count of seventy beats a minute of his natural ability to generate electricity and a pulse. In his head, he heard the voice of the man that came in times of his distress and caught the smell of antiseptic in the air. Calm down, the man said, in a warm and compassionate voice that seemed laced with hopes and with prayers from the heavens. He laid a tender hand on his head that put him to sleep.

This is a test, one that is meant to put you through your paces. If you can excel at this, you can excel at anything. Don't you worry; you're in very good care now, and I'll make sure of that, the man said. He pressed a metal ring against Christopher's chest; it was cold and sang a song with the beats of his heart.

The incoherency of his piccolo trumpet blared out and

reached him deep in his sleep; the music of Rudresh Mahanthappa and Steve Lehman played in the background. He heard The General and likened it to a circle being drawn in the middle of a Pollock, its wild colours of convergence like a hurricane going about the canvass. He made a mental note of the painting that he saw: the black against the scarcity of white that opposed, the savage red that portrayed depth and gore, the yellow in which he saw his optimism and his madness, and the blue expressing his serenity and health. He saw the face of DeSilva in the painting, smiling back at him with her ears pricked and her hair about the canvass.

It is you, again, he finally said, but the face simply smiled back at him. It is you from my dreams and without freedom.

It is you that brings about your own freedom, she finally said. I am merely a convergence, a thoroughbred in a field, like the oceans converging with the land, the sun burning in the heavens depicting the start of day, the turn of dusk before the moon comes out; like the colours you see at twilight, burnt orange and purple, a blue deep as the seas depicting the start of night, the meeting of two pittas on a branch and their symphony at dawn; like the very circle you envision on a Pollock, the big and the small, the swirls of wind and their turbulence, the contribution to the biosphere made by dung beetles feeding on horse dung, the barley straws and finest alfalfa masticated by the thoroughbred, the strength and might of oxygen-rich blood, all in one and the same gust of wind. It's here and then gone, just like the wind, she said.

And perhaps you can tell me whether I have taken one too many Amantadine. Have I taken too much Phenylpropanolamine? Have I mixed it too much for my kicks, the Benzodiazepine? Christopher asked, but the face of DeSilva in the painting simply smiled back. After a minute or two of not much but a fog in his head, he surrendered to the notion that all was as it was meant to be, a waking dream, and soon enough, he was awake and going about his business of tuning TV sets and soldering wires together in a shop in the hopes of chancing upon a signal.

Chapter 17.

The Simmer

Like the trickle of honey and the cool, gentle melt of chocolate in a pot, the drift of summer wind through an aperture and its caress of skin, the fresh, lingering chill of sub-Saharan mentha and its sweet kicks, the sizzle of calamine on a burn and a cold bathe in milk, he saw himself through the paces of surrender. He negotiated gravity with ease, a song about summer love playing in the background, and his body floated about the space of his room.

The Bombay, in a moderate temperament, licked its paws and gave itself a good clean. Then it curled up on the ledge and watched the drift of his body in the air. It remained indifferent and without a care or concern, its nature being to sleep at every inopportune hour of the day when the sun was at its most productive.

The notion of patience ran across Christopher's mind like a titan. A halo of rings circled round his head, and he witnessed his heart at peace for the very first time in his life. He found that all had been but an illusion of self, with a notion of self-loathing that he needed to get away from. Sleep had been his instrument of choice, although he hadn't known it or how he had managed to acquire the ability to make a mint. He had simply known that he was coming up with something and that his hand had been on the pulse, but this very something was slipping out of his grip like a thought in his head. It was there and then gone without a prompt.

The Bombay continued its nap until the hours of fine grain and salt. The shadows went about the ritual of their dance, never mimicking but rather enjoying voyeuristically his body palpitating about the space of his room. They smirked when he stopped, and as though he had gained their approval, they continued in their dance.

He simmered down and heard the voice of DeSilva. It is you, again, from my dreams, he said, but she simply smiled at him. She brushed through his hair and left him with the notion of a current flowing like a river through boulders, every stroke of her fingers feeling electric.

When she finally spoke, it was to say that she had been waiting for him, waiting for a time when he was ready. She knew of his every desire, from the food that he craved to his lust. She told him to imagine the moon over the sun and their production of a shadow. If it had been good enough for them to engage for only seven minutes, then he need not worry; the two shadows were simply doing as they should to be voyeurs of their physical being, even though they had never mimicked them, and when the time was right, their qualms would eventually fall to the ground.

The seed he needed to sow was his patience and give it the right amount of water. No seed can survive a drought, she said. It's all in the nurture.

He felt arousal in his groin and the flow of blood through his veins, the heat of the room and the heat of his blood, the heat in his chest and the quickened curiosity of the Bombay. Its eyes were as green as emeralds, and its coat as glossy as porcelain. The intensity of colours came alive in an instant, and the voice of DeSilva had heightened to a pitch. He witnessed the many faces of euphoria that she expressed to him, from her pain to her joy, her extremities of agony and pleasure, until she eventually collapsed onto the sweaty shore of his chest that had been as good as its weight in silver and gold.

He spoke only to confirm his satisfaction and that no single dose could have been good enough. Not even with the best of engineers at their disposal could they have formulated a construct as enduring as she had done with the brilliance of her sensibility and her use of reality.

All had seemed to him like a great piece of art, like a painting by a great creator, and himself a subject of it, a man in a grave state in a dream of Ferdinand Hodler. He considered the possibility that he might be in one of those dreams, dreams of men in faraway states, their hopes and aspirations a distant memory with only a lingering shred of benevolence to accompany them through the dead of the night.

When the tides of enigma subsided and he was able to pull together two decent strings of reasoning, he concluded that it could only have been in his dreams and there alone.

Chapter 18.
A story about Matsukawa

Woman of the coats: I hear ripples. They are faint, but I hear them.

Good, replied Yamamoto Kasuga, the storekeeper.

Chiyoko's palms rested upon the black and white keys of a grand piano. They perspired at every moment that Yamamoto doled out instructions to the boy. He felt the smoothness of the ivory, and the glossy black piano captured a perplexed reflection of himself sitting in wait. He took note of the gold, spiral lettering saying *Steinway & Sons*.

You sit and watch – it will come, said the storekeeper. She is never too late, always beneath the surface, and this is the most uncomfortable truth about her, he said in an accent of the Nagaoka prefecture. Mind always has to be empty – this is the only way.

It was late October, by his estimation. He watched the autumn leaves on the trees, orange and red from the hills of Matsuguchi, near the place where his father had buried a Bonin fox. He heard a loud bang on the door and hurriedly hid behind a large winter coat. The scent of old rose in a vase of aged lavender water lingered with a hint of musk and sandalwood. He heard Yamamoto and his explanation of the woman who would come, and in due time she would inspire him to be a great pianist.

Chiyoko Matsukawa reimagined himself as a little boy lost in the woods, the tall slender trees of Matsuguchi that neighboured the hills of Bijin Bayashi. I wish I could be lost within those tall beauties, he thought, and in their midst I would be safe. He heard a man grumbling outside and recognized it as the same voice from a fortnight ago when three crows had had a spat over a dead carcass. Watching from his bedroom window, he noticed the crow's large beaks and a show for dominance. Each had a dig into the rotten carcass of the Bonin fox in the most natural display of brutalism. He watched them dance about the carcass on two little feet, their beaks wide open, fluttering about to chase off the other crows.

He heard the voice of the man, faint and dreamy, his words diffracted through the walls. Where have they gone? he heard the man say to a semblance of his father projected onto a shoji. The paper wall made him appear to be hanging onto life by a single thread, and the flame of a candle made him seem even more ghostly than he ought to have been at that moment. You cannot hide them from us, the man said. If you've come to these hills to hide, it is a poor choice on your part and an even weaker decision than your last. Tokyo is a big city; if we could find you there, I am sure we can find you anywhere. We know where you live, where you take your morning walks and your coffee runs, the park where you take your dog out for a walk in the mornings. The man spoke in the withered Japanese of the region of Kyushu.

We give you three days. In three days, if we have heard nothing from you, then our decision is final: we take the boy. In three days, if we have heard nothing, the boy comes with us.

From where he hid behind the winter coats, Chiyoko heard the haunting voice of the man, its timbre ravaged by the bad habits of cigarette smoking and whiskey drinking, gravelly like boots on a shore in winter. He felt a shiver down his spine. In three days… Chiyoko listened with his ears pressed against the wood that amplified the man's voice. The volume frightened him; he knelt, submissive to the dread, and remembered being lifted high in the arms of his father. It seemed to him that the end was near. The men's conversation was about large funds that had gone missing. The lead hontoni was smoking a joint, the smell of which made its way into the wardrobe where he hid. He barked out an order to his men, after which they departed into the dark.

It's okay, the lady said. It's okay, Chiyoko, you can come out.

He heard the slam of a car door and the quiet rattle of its engine starting. He heard the car pull away from the drive and exit the lot, its headlights straying through the gap in the wood.

It's okay, you can come out, she urged the boy gently. Chiyoko pushed past the heavy, scented coats and reached for the handle. He was welcomed by a subtle smile and arms wide open like the banks of a river and an embrace from the woman.

He remembered her scent and her kimono and how it had given in to him. He walked into her embrace and recollected the woman's hair fallen over her face and how smooth it was when he had tried to grasp it, how it had slipped out of his hands and behind her back. He wrapped his arms around the woman as far as he could and watched the dark curtain of her hair cover his face, protecting him from a danger that had long gone. He remembered her perfume of bergamot and jasmine, a hint of orange wrapped in a quadrant of saturated geese fat, the long draw of liquorice and a punch of ylang ylang oil. Chiyoko stayed within the woman's bosom long enough to pick up the musk of burnt hazelnuts in whiskey casked in pinewood. There he buried himself, looking through the strands of the woman's hair, and fought with the notion of fear.

That woman's name was Yamatoshi Ito.

Chapter 19.
Tokyo

Are we going back to Tokyo? Chiyoko Matsukawa asked Yamatoshi Ito. Her hair was over his face, and his lungs were struggling for oxygen. He made a gap in the curtain of her hair so he could breathe; a puff and a half was all that he needed. He allowed himself to remain in the comfort of her bosom.

Cherry blossom will be upon us soon, Yamamoto Ito said. We'll catch the first break from the snow. They were only metres away from his father's Okina ie. The forest was moist with dew, and the wild shrubs persistently scratched his ankles. The clouds parted as they walked. Yamamoto Ito kept a constant guard, like a scout, to avoid being spotted as they moved. It was late evening, with a lethargic moon hovering above them.

Chiyoko Matsukawa witnessed himself as an adolescent with all of his possessions in a bag and a Shonen Manga series, Kotaro Makaritoru Volume II, clutched against his abdomen. The whispering of Bijin Bayashi was in his ears. They were surrounded by the majestic wonder of slender trees, a lowered lavender sky, the chirps of crickets brushing their teeth in a quest for a mate, and the broken pretence of desolate silence created by the forest. Their tread was gentle upon the ground, and they watched carefully for anything that could make a noise.

Are we going back to Tokyo? Chiyoko asked a distracted Yamamoto Ito, with her gaze in the woods and her ears to the birds. If they stayed awake, they were sure to alert to her to any threat. Who were those men? Chiyoko asked. Will my father come to join us? he pressed a distant Yamatoshi Ito.

Hontoni, Yamatoshi Ito snapped. They are very dangerous men. Dangerous, but in Tokyo you will be safe. She returned to wrestling with the shrubs and making a pathway. We stay alive this way, she said.

Chapter 20.

Cinnamon Girl

When Christopher woke, it was to the brilliance of evergreen. He witnessed the display of Otto strength from the thoroughbred; when the horse's hooves struck the earth, it echoed with ripples of force. He witnessed his incessant desire fixated on the horse's muscles like flies on an ointment. It wasn't a desire for consummation but to adopt its strength. Where his weakness had been profound, the beast offered an inspiration of chutzpah, a symbol of absolute vigour.

Regardless, this too would pass. He allowed the thought to do away with him. When he regained consciousness, it was to the voice of a woman in his head. Do you remember? she asked him. Do you remember the two pittas and their toots in the early hours of the morning? It would be pleasing to me if you did, so pleasing to me if you would remember?

But he hadn't remembered her, not in the way she wanted to be remembered. Instead, he saw her as a face in a crowd. He recognised her but not as she wanted him to. She seemed to him to be somehow drawn out of something aged, revealed like some sort of alluring apogee. She smelt like a faded rose in a vase of aged lavender water, with a hint of musk and sandalwood, like the scent of another man on her.

The cracks on the walls of mould grew and oozed bacteria, which smelt like sulphur. He paid attention to the shadows and the way that they moved about the space of his room, not mimicking them but holding smiles on their faces, and the voyeur-like porcelain statues watching as the woman danced above his torso until he became free in mind and in spirit. What inevitably stayed with him the most was why the woman kept appearing in his dreams as though he had converged with her soul.

The young girl ran down the stairs into a garden of Galilean temperament and cut through the hedges of olive. She obtained an audience with the gathered horses, whilst the young boy counted down to one, with his eyes obediently shut. He had buried them in his palms and wished for the time when he would be able to count proficiently; the task would be much easier if he could quickly get down to the number one.

She had taught him how to count one number after the other. The larger number first, she said, then the smaller one. You think of the bigger number first, like ten, and then you count the smaller one, nine, she said, then the number eight and seven and six. You see it's just like counting upwards except you're counting downwards until you get to the number one. Don't forget to close your eyes! You have to close your eyes – it's the rules. If you open them, that's cheating, and you're not a cheat, are you? The boy said nothing. Then don't open your eyes when you count. You have to promise me this, she said. Promise me you will only open your eyes and come looking for me once you've counted down to one, she said. Now promise me.

He started to count and only stopped to second guess himself. He thought that he might have missed a certain number, and that would be unfair to the girl, so he recounted: nine, eight, seven, he counted, careful not to skip any numbers. He wondered how smart the girl was and how she had become so proficient with numbers at such a young age; she rattled them off as she pleased. She was unlike him. His whole world had been at war with numbers from the day he was born to the present moment at an age a little over ten years old.

The ginkgo tree stood majestically and there he counted, facing the tree trunk. He wondered whether she could hear him calling out each number hesitantly. He was quiet for a while and took in the present moment with a deep breath before continuing. Seven, six, five, Christopher counted out loud to the running girl in search of a place to hide. She ran as fast as she could through the thorns of the hedge and the wire fence. She ran past the bird cage where two pittas chirped in hysteria at her presence. She thought of wings and how she would fly and cover miles of ground, although she ignored the fact that the same birds were trapped in a cage and their wings were useless except to give them a lift from one man-made metal branch to the next. He never caught me, she thought, eying their wings and the romance of the two love birds none the wiser about their caged predicament.

Christopher continued to count. He reached deep and projected his voice out into the air. Before the next number, he wondered where the girl had hidden – in the bush of thorn, perhaps, or the hollow path, the dark tunnel of hedge that led nowhere, he thought.

She settled her feet deep in the salt, her shoes soaked in the mud. She listened out for the boy, sure that he would be put off by the prowl of dragonflies at the entrance. The mere sight of darkness was enough to overwhelm him, she reasoned a thousand times, until an idea whizzed into her head. He was sure to peek, she was sure of it, by the time he called out the number one; she had already begun a furloughed existence in an imaginary place, sitting with her feet steeped deep in the mud.

Chapter 21.
Whiskey

Christina DeSilva heard the dried cress leaves breaking. She heard his footsteps, organic, as they came through the cold. She heard the warmth of his diction as he called out to her, in contrast to her desolate hiding place. One… I'm coming to look for you! the boy shouted in excitement at his turn to play in the game.

She had hoped it would take him longer, longer so that she could give herself up to the persuasion of her daydreams.

She heard the rattle of an empty drum which the boy was kicking about. She heard how it gave a hollow sound, empty of its whiskey that had been the man's haven and his downfall and led to the early death of his aspirations. She had hoped he would make something of himself, perhaps a brilliant jazz player or a music director.

She dreamt of him as he danced naked, in nothing but his briefs and socks, the excitement of his muscles and the salt of his sweat and the steam of the heat he generated in the harsh summer day, all of which dampened his soul as he drank. She saw him fall to the ground in exhaustion, his spirit renewed and cleansed of impurity. This was how she saw the man whom she loved.

She knew Christopher Myen had to be near as she had heard the shudder of barrels where the thoroughbred fed on the finest alfalfa blended with barley that had fallen to the ground. In the autumn, these barrels were used to collect rainwater for the horses to drink. It was good for their bones and free of chlorine that destroyed their teeth. She heard Christopher Myen as he followed the path that led to the bird cage where the pittas fluttered and chirped.

Earlier that morning, Christina DeSilva, at the age of twelve, had had a certain premonition of herself and could already see her life in the future with a man she would love. It came to her instinctively as a sort of future reading like tarot cards, her knowledge of all the man's flaws and his weaknesses, his strengths and his passion for music. She knew it down to the minutest detail and came to the conclusion that most people did not deserve the bad things that happened to them but rather they experienced a certain sort of unfortunate coincidence.

In her daydream, she allowed the revelations of her life to simply flow, neither forced nor chased, aware of the notion of chasing a golden goose. She saw herself as a mature woman and beautiful in all her glory. She reframed herself, away from all judgement, and simply allowed her day dreams to depict her as they wished; when they revealed to her a fallen intoxication with a man drowned in an obsession with liquid spirits, she gave no further thought to it. She thought of herself simply as the whiskey and the source of the man's downfall. She later thought herself as also the source of the man's joy, dark and malty and with the strength of inebriety that left him on the floor for days.

In all senses, she needed nothing in her dreams except to fulfil a burning desire, the pursuit of a man, a fallen one. It was as though she had lost all desire for everything in life and been reduced to her most primal state, with no drive and content simply to exist. Later, she saw herself on the opposite side of her obsession, wealthy and with so many acquired possessions that they overburdened her. They were like a protection against her insecurities and an escape from her reality. She sat in the bushes, bewildered by the sudden euphoria and the realisation that what would eventually happen would happen and nothing she attempted would ever change the outcome. She surrendered herself to her revelations and leaned into them. She made her problems as domesticated as a house pet, knowing full well the extent of their poison but reassured by the comfort of the known.

The boy, walking in the footsteps of grace and wandering with serendipity, stumbled upon the place where she had hidden. I know where you are, he called out. I know where you are hiding – behind these shrubs. I can see you, he said. You can come out now.

The girl kept quiet and embraced a cool, gentle demeanour. She tucked her legs against her chest, in high hopes the boy was chancing his luck. There was no way he could have found her here, she thought, here in the dark. The more she thought about it, the more it bothered her. She wished she could break free and simply take to the skies, fly like the two pittas, embraced by the wind under their wings and their beady eyes gleaming with ecstasy.

She wrestled with the notion of freedom and placed it on a Libra scale, but it simply outweighed the most basic of her reasoning. What, truly, is freedom? she pondered, in the midst of mud and salt and the musky, sweet scent of fallen leaves piled on the ground where she had hidden.

If it came down to it, were the pitta birds free? Held within caged parameters, they simply fluttered from one branch to the next in the hope that their world would eventually get bigger. If they lived long enough, would they exert themselves? she wondered. Break free of their cage or surrender to a caged fate? I once saw a bird standing in its cage with the door wide open; it had made a home of it cage. Perhaps this is me, she thought.

Chapter 22.
The Pact

Later that evening, Christina DeSilva took to her bed, ill with the flu. She had been full of life earlier that morning, enjoying the first fresh autumn breeze on her face. Now she shivered constantly, gripping a swirl of feathery nothingness, and her head had become something of a feverish adventure.

She witnessed herself running through the yard as the boy counted down from ten, facing the rough bark of the gingko tree, unsure of himself and wondering whether he had counted right.

She witnessed the ease of the breeze that blew across her face, the sweet musk of fallen leaves from the gingko trees and the runway of dried cress that brushed against her feet as she ran. She contemplated the boy's choice of a place to hide, hearing screams of old following her to outcompete the sounds of the plants around her ankles, their psithurism only second base to her sense of flight.

When it was her turn to count, she called out the numbers precisely. Sanguine in imaginary episodes of flight, she thought only of the possibility of taking to the air like the pittas had done and doing away with the dread diagnosis that had occupied her mind for most of her life. She buried her head in her palms and counted just as the boy had done, her eyes in a world of darkness and her palms inducing a tolerable warmth, assured of her ability to count downwards.

Christopher's thumb was bleeding from a cut from a thorn and she knew instantly what to do. She took the boy's hand, placed his thumb in her mouth and sucked it to apply pressure and stop the bleeding. It came to her that it was odd to say that part of him was now in her. She tasted how metallic his blood was on her tongue. It's your turn now, she said. She cut herself on a thorn of the wax shrub and waited for it to bleed. You suck it and you swallow – at least, I think that's how it's done, she said.

She expected her blood would taste of metal, too. She placed her thumb on the boy's lips. You lick it, she said. See… that way we can be together, she added.

But I don't want to lick your blood, the boy objected. It's your blood – you lick it.

I licked yours, she insisted. It's my blood – you lick it, she ordered the boy, who was half way to discovering green lust for the girl and being overwhelmed by the confusion of falling in love with her. You can be so ungrateful sometimes, the girl said. I helped you out with yours. Now you can help me with mine. And for the very first time in her life, she noticed how much she wanted someone to be a part of her. You can lick it like I licked yours, she insisted. That way, we can be together.

Just like in the movies? asked the boy.

Yes, just like in the movies, replied the girl.

Christina DeSilva allowed the moment to exist just as she wanted it to. She watched the boy as he raised no further objection to her, then recounted the taste of her blood, certain the same metal taste of hers would serenade on his tongue.

Now we've made a pact, she said.

Now what? asked the boy.

Well… now we play, the girl said, delighted in her ability to persuade the boy.

Their feet soon raced about the ground, scattering mud off their shoes onto the concrete and then onto the raised floor of wood, until they eventually paused on the porcelain that had been the brilliance of Moroccan influence.

Eight, the girl counted, sure that the boy would run in search of a new place to hide. She took in the dark patterns of the tiles and admired their form. That afternoon, the sun came down on the stones and showcased their true likeness. They weren't a singular black but a multiplicity of hues that made up the black, a polished topaz and a plethora of greys. She had been to the house several times before, although it hadn't occurred to her to observe the floor where she stood. She would simply wait for the boy as he got ready; neither did the boy ever give her time to become impatient enough to observe her surroundings.

Seven, she called out to the boy, certain he would have hidden somewhere as she could no longer hear his feet stomping about the grounds of the house. Five, she called out in the company of the Bombay, with its tail lifted high into air as it brushed against her leg; it always did that to leave a scent, both of affection and of territory.

When Christina finished her count, she walked towards the door and entered a room. Not far behind her was the Bombay, playing a game of its own. It crossed in between her legs and beckoned for attention. Well then, baba, she said, you wouldn't mind telling me where you think he would be hiding now, would you? The Bombay was long, stretched into a purr and a call to be fed.

She held the cat by its ears and gave it a good rub to calm it down. Now I wish I had your good fortune, she said, and allowed the cat to flee out of her hands onto a ledge where it looked back at her with dissatisfaction.

Chapter 23.

Float

In the midst of the Bombay's dissatisfaction with self, it nursed on its stomach as it grumbled on two pennies of thought. With the scent of ammonia in the air from mould growth and bad ventilation, the delusion provided by the faintly cracked walls that Christopher saw before him and the reassurance of familiarity that his bedroom offered him, he found himself not hiding in a place but rather at home, and not ten years of age but rather grown into the full sense of manhood. He was in his bed where he witnessed the drift of shadows as they made pilgrimage on his walls in a way that could only be described as close to benevolence when they took to the air and held smiles of reverence on their faces.

His landlord had said that the whispers of old had made good of his bad deeds, so he kept his profits before his duties and kept his goodwill in a cage like a bird which he released every now and then for leverage; he referred to this as a good trap, one to keep him in his tenancy.

Christopher weighed up these episodes of feverish nights when everything had seemed a hallucination, from the shadows on his wall and their drift into the air to their climb onto the blinds that poorly shielded his room from the moonlight. A second time he witnessed the shadows rise into the air and reach for his clothing. He witnessed their playful ways and how they examined their silhouette in the mirror. While he was fast asleep in his dreams, the shadows watched the rhythm of his breathing and the cold sweats of his body.

Christopher Myen thought these visions could not really be happening and only in his dreams were there the illusions of shadows and talking pitta birds. Outside, the moon had shone with absolute brilliance, as bright as daylight itself.

The smell of fresh dung drifted in from three doors down where a thoroughbred chewed on leftover straw. His eyes were in a wilderness of borrowed promises and his head buried deep underneath his pillow of graded goose down.

If I could only let myself catch them, he said, these fleeting visions. I did return to her, but what are these things floating about the space? No sleep and no letting light in, not if I can help it, he said to himself. He twisted his head so it faced the stile door next to the window where the moon was perfectly centred, hugged by the window's frame like a portrait of a white dot on black canvass, like a small boat going out to sea. Christopher managed to whisk himself away to someplace visceral, a place of mirrored isomers, where he stayed afloat in his sleep.

Is this what you wanted? he heard one Christina DeSilva

ask. He heard her at her most viral, as he hadn't done before. Is this what you wanted? she asked of him a second time. Her tone was heavy and her presence ever more prurient. He felt her hands around his throat as though forcing a word out of him, but none came. He felt the cold of his tongue and the mist of his breath and the pressure on his vocal cords, but none came. He felt heaviness below his waist and a word on his mind, but none came. Not a single word, he thought to himself; not from the many thousands that raced about his mind. He thought of a few chosen words, the sort of thinking one does to separate reality from dreams. When he finally managed to speak, it was through clouds that floated out of his mouth into the air like cotton.

There she was like a beam of light, instantly put together and formed. He thought of her as a moment that was here and then gone in an instant. He chose to keep his eyes open and watched her. He thought only of her nature and how almost Presbyterian she seemed to him, with her hint of western sub-Saharan features and her womanhood and the way that she disassociated herself from time and form.

When the familiarity of dusk returned, he managed to pull himself a degree of reasoning. He pondered thoughts and strung along enquiries like dominoes collapsing in a line. How did you come to be here with me? Did you want this too, yours as well as mine? he heard in a voice like Christina DeSilva's. Christopher witnessed the leaping shadows on his wall and followed them one last time as they danced around his bedpost. It seemed to him as though a ritual of some sort was being conducted, commensurate with the long wait. When Christina DeSilva's face appeared, she had become pale as water. He didn't recognise her, not as he had known her when she was young, in her virtue, before she had bled. The face above him was new, with the subtlety of a smile as she intended it.

Why were you so difficult? she whispered the whole time. Why was it so difficult for you to end up here with me? Her ears became moist from her cold breath, and her eyes remained still as dusk, withstanding the frost that had accompanied her.

Christina DeSilva made herself into a flame of undying plasma so that his room became alive and gave him the chance to glance at her delicacy as she had intended, pale petals in a garden of wild bush ferns. H gazed for a while at the body of Christina DeSilva, mature in all the glory and virtue of womanhood.

I thought you were gone, she whispered. Left me here all by myself. It's quite lonely here, she added. Christopher sank into a pool of his own rush; his eyes narrowed into a sluggish stare and his cerebellum released an explosion of illusions, one being the thoroughbreds chewing on the most exquisite of barley straw until their heads imploded.

Any sound would do, he thought. The pressure below…

You don't have to tell me – I knew you were coming, he heard the voice of Christina DeSilva say to him. Do you remember the aviary? she asked. Well… of course. Why would you?

An old rose in a vase of aged lavender water, sweet and fresh as the barley straw, lingered long with a hint of musk and sandalwood and a spark down his spine, and at least a minute passed. Then he recognised her scent: it was that of a woman. He thought of her muscles as they pulled and relaxed against his veins and the monotonous way in which they pushed against his groin. Her hair ran down her breast and left a corridor of flesh as pristine as though it had never once been kissed by the sun. Her lower bits flowed to a point; they dangled above his chest like tentacles, engendering a ripple that sent shockwaves as they brushed against his chest. Can you see me? she asked him. Can you feel me? she whispered into his ears and left them cold and moist as decaying remnants after a massacre. Her moans became so sharp that they pierced the air and left a trace of amber rose. His arms lay by his sides, and he was oblivious to their weight until the intensity reached him deep in his head.

Christopher Myen fought a losing battle and drowned himself in the decibels of Christina Desilva's moans. His torso was covered in goose pimples from the sinful dance she gave him, erect as plants drawing towards the afternoon sun and as smooth as python's skin. When the chill of the night came knocking, it came as unannounced as tax collectors with the workings of mathematics far beyond common comprehension.

She calculated with ease the vigorousness of her movement above him. The rattling of the blinds became louder and outcompeted her, so she wailed even louder. The chair that had been next to the rail where his clothes had hung seemed to levitate; the lamp by the bed post loosened slowly from the electric socket into which it was plugged and took to the air. A deathly silence followed until everything in his room was up in the air in a state of inertia.

Do you? I mean really, do you? Christina DeSilva asked, but Christopher's tongue remained heavy.

I can hear you, but I can't utter a word. I force it, but nothing comes. Perhaps you can release me, release me just as you've collapsed into me? he thought.

The two shadows were back as voyeurs, afloat but not mimicking them, just as lovers, muted and dark, and the familiarity of his room returned to him.

Chapter 24.
Morning Glory

Drenched in sweat, Christopher Myen was much out of his rhythm. A strong musk billowed through the room where he laid his head. He picked up the scent of old rose, he listened to the rattle of the blind in the wind and he saw the pittas long drifted into a sleep of their own, with their heads buried beneath their wings and their chests in the air.

Christopher Myen listened to the voice and dismissed it as the sort of talk that comes to one when in deep sleep. It really couldn't have been that real, I mean none of it, he thought. He worked his eyes around the room and found it to be the same as before, the chair next to the rail and the lamp still plugged into its socket, his clothing hanging neatly on the rail next to the blinds that gently shifted with every breeze against the window.

As far as he could remember, something unwise had happened. According to his judgement, none of it was in moderation: her being there at dusk, the first time it had happened, seeing what seemed like two fireflies in the dark and their floating about the space of his room, their coordinates of synchrony and their lust for flesh at dusk. He witnessed the brightness of her pearls, a rendition of a woman's smile, and her silhouette hugged by the moon's candescence. It dawned on him that he might not be dreaming but awake, witnessing the manifestation of one Christina DeSilva owning and over his torso. He heard the sounds of a day's long celebration dwindle into the night and a semblance of his mother's voice, quiet and plummy. He remembered it being the night of his tenth celebration of life and the gift of a kiss he'd received, cold and gently pressed against his cheeks. He remembered his lips being moist as she parted from him. You will remember this, DeSilva had said; then she'd faded away into a mist.

The year before, Christina DeSilva had taken to her bed and passed away. For weeks, she had been burning with a fever, and a day before she expired, she noticed the emergence of cold sores around her mouth, the stiffness of her neck and the taste of metal ore on her tongue. The temperature of her head had risen to a boil.

A few weeks before, Christina DeSilva had run around the yard, breaking through the autumn morning chill and making the pittas in their cage hysterical with a stick. I'll learn to fly someday, she had said to the birds, just like you two. It was lost on her that the two pittas had never flown out of their cage or experienced the open air against their wings.

She was always one little sick girl, our Christina, her mother sobbed to the physician, who loaned an ear of sympathy and a vice of patience to the woman whilst the girl's father rubbed her back, in too much pain at the sudden loss of their daughter.

Two weeks after Christina DeSilva's passing, Christopher Myen stood at the spot in the yard where they had often played. He watched the two pittas eating a worm out of the mud and fighting with their bills. He sat in the company of the Bombay cat, so worn out with worry that it later curled up in his lap and fell asleep. He looked into the sky and saw the circling of a hawk in the brightness of the afternoon sun; nearby were the hawk's nestlings desperate to be fed, their cries like those of a human baby, hoping for the mangled body of an animal strangled by the hawk's talons. He fell asleep with the Bombay curled up in his lap. Far into his sleep, he heard the whispers of the likeness of one Christina DeSilva. The clock struck twelve, she said, and I had lost you. I saw you at the base of my bed whilst I was fighting – did you see me? I fought as hard as I could, she whispered into his moist, alkaline ears, half-dead to the world. I just couldn't pull through. I couldn't beat it – I really tried. I saw your face at the base of my bed, my mother's too. My poor Mona! I wish I could have said bye to her. During this time she became a broken woman, but your face I held on to. It was the last thing that withered away with me, she whispered.

As the ventilator went about its business, it made a frantic noise that induced panic in the nurse; her utensil clattered about in a bowl which she held close to her chest, a sure sign of her inexperience in the profession. The TV lost its signal and gave off a white noise that reached Christopher deep in his sleep. He puzzled over his existence and the events that had brought him to a place full of pistons and pressure bags intent on retaining life in bodies. The smell of antiseptic lingered in the air. He heard the deep voice of a man, astute although without understanding. He hadn't been as damaged as the man had proclaimed. According to him, he had been well and in good spirits, sitting on a bench with a Bombay taking a nap on his lap. He's coming back to us! he heard the lady say to the man, and he listened more.

Let me have a look at that, the physician said to the nurse. Sadly not; he's having another one of his episodes. Keep an eye on the bird, the physician said, showing his age and experience. His PSP should be within 5 to 8 litres per minute, in Respiratory Minute Volume, that is. If he goes beyond this, you get me right on the phone immediately, he ordered. The others are quite stable, but the same goes for them, too. An eye on the bird and keep a log, he added. Concur?

I concur.

As it pulsated at a higher rate than normal, a hundred and twenty-two beats per minute, the nurse made a note, her eyes fixed on the heart-rate monitor.

Chapter 25.
Woman-god

When faraway thoughts didn't come easy to Christopher, he held onto hopes of an approaching voice in the dark; if the woman's whispered puzzles confused him, he tossed tens of times in his bed, expecting the fatigue to whisk him away into sleep. When that didn't work, he thought about the phenomenon of counting sheep in the dark. I'll count the sheep, imaginary as they are, and watch as they leap out of the fog and over the clouds in my head… One sheep, he began to count, and bet on a break in the wind that he would eventually fall asleep. There I will meet the woman again, he thought, of the likeness to one Christina DeSilva. Two and three, expecting the dull task to win and draw him away into sleep. There it would be dark, and the woman would appear to him in her most comfortable state and her purest essence.

The whistling of wind broke through the blind, showing a glimpse of the vast open landscape where his body was laid, covered in white linen. His eyes closed peacefully, a damp cloth placed upon his forehead gently taking the heat away. The place was serene, and a calculated drop of saline went through his veins. She smiled at him. It's you again. I wondered when I would see you again, he heard the voice of the woman say to him. I only see you when you sleep a good sleep.

Losing himself to the dark and finding himself before the woman, he realised she was there not of her own accord but by the precursor of his imagination, contrived, controlled and limited in her bearing like a broken record on replay or the buffering of a browser struggling to find a domain address. He later let go of his ambitions and simply fell without a course or concern. When he woke, he found himself standing in front of a mirror. It was afternoon by his calculation and the sun had begun a solitary burn. In the mirror, he saw himself a youth of about ten years of age staring back at him without a word, as though waiting for an order or instruction from a mature version of himself.

Occasionally he would hear life going by outside his window, the birds chirping in the trees and the wind dropping in the evening, and draw the conclusion that all wasn't as it was meant to be, transient and ever-evolving. He woke a second time to find himself in a ball, encapsulated in walls of his own self-delusion, his mind on a wave like a seesaw going up and down for minutes on end. When it eventually stopped, it was to a vision of himself playing his brass piccolo Bb, blowing into the trumpet with his guts, with the music of the legendary Chiyoko Matsukawa delicate in the background.

The music of Chiyoko Matsukawa was played in a minor key and elicited the likeness of one Christina DeSilva from him. He heard her voice in his head and his music in his heart and went about playing without direction, simply letting the lure of the woman take precedence over his will and surrendering to her every whim.

When he dreamt, it was of her telling him how wonderful he was and how she had made a genius out of him, until she dissipated into a mist. He kept at his embouchure until the remainder of her dissipated in him like the residues of diamorphine in his veins.

Chapter 26.

Shared Illusion

Christopher woke up a third time and found Chiyoko Matsukawa at his Steinway & Sons playing Ludwig van Beethoven's Piano Concerto No 3. It had puzzled him why he had been in his adolescence and why a strange man had stood by his side guarding him as his fingers went along the black and white keys; when he missed a note, the man prompted him to start over.

He stood in the shadows and watched Chiyoko Matsukawa playing solo to a concerto piece as though the moments had already been seen, and with every revision, it dawned on him that he might have taken one too many of his prescribed Amantadine for the flu and might have mixed it with an earlier prescription of Phenylpropanolamine. With shaky legs, he got out of bed and walked the length of his room to where a basin was installed. He saw the cracks on the walls and his blind opened to the elements, letting a gentle breeze in. At the basin, he pulled open the cabinet above and rummaged around a clutter of brown bottles, reaching for one labelled Benzodiazepine. He let the water pour from the tap, closed it, then counted the loose droplets that leaked from the pipe afterwards until it measured a crown full. He threw back a pill and swallowed it; he listened for the dead sound and waited for the 0.5mg of Benzodiazepine to kick in.

Perhaps another one, he heard what sounded like the voice of Chiyoko Matsukawa. I could do with one myself. These moods have overtaken me. It's strange. I listened and I heard you, too, the voice said. I was hell bent – I've been mad for days. Christopher turned to catch glimpse of the ghost but it had gone like a thought in his head. He threw back another pill and waited for the kick. Another should do it. I, too, could do with one, he heard the voice say.

Chiyoko, is that you? Christopher called out. Chiyoko, he repeated, and waited for the familiarity of dead sound but instead caught the gentle breeze that badgered the blinds into a conversation between two different materials. Chiyoko, Christopher repeated. I must be going mad. I swear I heard the voice of Matsukawa.

Well, she crashed into me, too, he finally heard, but not as she did to you.

Chiyoko, is that you? I swear I heard your voice, almost as though I was approaching mania. Is that you, Chiyoko? Have I seen a ghost? Christopher waited for about a minute to pass, by his calculations, as he listened to the droplets from the tap. When nothing came back in the way of the voice of Matsukawa, he pushed on. Whatever are you doing here, and who's crashed into you? The lady as well? Has she done to you what she did to me? I am embarrassed to say these last few days have been full of bad dreams for me, he said to the faint shadow of Matsukawa standing by the door. Give me your hand as my legs are shaky bent and the benzos have had a field day with me. I can't seem to take a good leap at you. You wouldn't mind if I... He reached for the ghost of Chiyoko Matsukawa tucked into a fragment of dark, but when he took measured steps towards Chiyoko, he seemed further away. You wouldn't mind if I... Christopher asked again. Give me your hand – these floors are bent. And what is it that you carry on you, that scent of old rose in a vase of aged lavender water?

Of Ferdinand Hodler's, Chiyoko responded, and of the woman with a rose lost in contemplation.

The painter and the dream. Ferdinand Hodler – whatever has he got to do with this? Christopher asked.

I assure you, as a parallel, everything. She was on top, wasn't she? Chiyoko said.

Yes, she was just like in the painting, but what has it got to do with this? It couldn't have been the same girl, could it? Christopher asked.

Well, did her hair dance a good dance? he asked.

Yes, it did over her breast, but it couldn't have been, could it?

Perhaps it was, perhaps it wasn't. Perhaps Ferdinand was also inspired by her, and perhaps that's why she has also chosen to bother you?

I turned ten when it started to happen, precisely on the eve when DeSilva's face strongly resembled the woman's. It's almost as though I have been duped into something unworldly, although it could also be nothing but an illusion.

Well, if it's nothing, then why does it bother you?

Her undulating above and me paralysed below, just like in the painting, Christopher said.

Just like in the painting? Chiyoko replied.

Yes, just like in the painting of The Dream. The Dream, Chiyoko, it's incredibly parallel. Give me your hand; these floors are soft and they are sinking. Chiyoko! Christopher called. I can see you standing there in the dark, married to it like a bride. Now give me your hand, Chiyoko, Christopher called out. Matsukawa!

Chapter 27.

Electricity

A jolt of a volt passed through Chiyoko Matsukawa's body. Lights dazzled and mesmerised him into a colloquial outburst in a Japanese dialect originating in the region of Niigata. He recollected the lethargy of lights that blinked endlessly and the language in his head. He himself was lost to a space that was entirely white in colour but later included a variety of other colours. He heard the noise of a bustling city outside, and when he opened his eyes, he found himself in a busy Tokyo district.

The voices in his head persisted and made him think about Yamatoshi Ito. He heard her say to him that all would be well and that he needn't worry; the three men of Hontoni would be gone soon and they would be able to make their escape. He should stay put, and in due time, it would be safe for them to make their move from his father's Okina ie and the mountains of Matsuguchi.

Chiyoko Matsukawa witnessed the movement of the three men of Hontoni as they wobbled out the paper door like harp seals on ice and their cautionary declaration which lingered long in the air, as weighty as a bad smell. In three days, the lead Hontoni had said and turned a cold back riffed with disdain to a silhouette of his father, consumed by shame and grateful for a strand of mercy that had been granted upon his life.

In times of prosperity, Masatoshi Matsukawa had been a man of steadfast character, unwavering in his quest for quick gains. His gambling had been undeniably fruitful, and the same appetite for risk had offered him no shortfall in business. It was not until his deficit with the Inagawa-Kai that it seemed to the world that his betting had finally been to his detriment.

When it came to measurable risk, Masatoshi Matsukawa had the paws of Tough Claws. He bet hugely on instinct and won big, and when he placed on a whim, it usually resulted in big wins, too. The man seemed to be lose-proof.

Masatoshi's merchant enterprise became wildly profitable over the passing years, despite blatant difficulties. It was due to his unwavering dogma that he instilled in the plethora of shipmen that had come, mastered the skills and inevitably departed out of spite, down to the vessel's engine-men. As the shipment of strawberries was sure to result in stock losses and the best of the merchantmen would steer away from such endeavours, this was where Masatoshi Matsukawa excelled. He employed his creativity to ensure the preservation of his perishable cargo, most of which came from shores in the tropics, roughing the rogue waves that put the best of merchantmen to the test.

As sure as the Indian Ocean was bound to be choppy, Masatoshi Matsukawa was certain to be triumphant over the turbulence of the waves. He brought back to his home shores of Niigata fresh produce that was distributed as far afield as the city of Tokyo. He sold mainly to middlemen across the Niigata, Honshu and Tokyo regions. This made Masatoshi Matsukawa a very wealthy man.

Chiyoko Matsukawa listened with his ears pressed against the wood, scared stiff a samurai might, at any moment, be reincarnated. In three days, he heard, paralysed by the thought of his father's head on a plate and the squirt of blood as it pulsed out of his veins.

You can come out now, he heard Yamatoshi Ito say, with full assurance that her bosom would be a place of refuge for the boy when she wrapped him in the warmth of her embrace and cloaked him in her musk of bergamot, jasmine and freesia, a quadrant of apricot and orange saturated in geese fat and a whiff of liquorice steeped in a punch of ylang ylang. It's safe now, Yamatoshi Ito said. You can come out now, Chiyoko, she said in the Japanese of the Niigata region. Your father will be waiting for you, and Yamamoto Kasuga asked me to take you to him, Yamatoshi Ito added. A young Chiyoko Matsukawa walked out the cupboard, comfortable as cotton. He nestled his right palm in Ito's left, and she led him through a corridor of cryptomeria and cypress, assured that the rattle of wood insects was unlikely to unsettle the boy.

Chiyoko Matsukawa met with his father, who stood in the dim light of his study, sombre as dusk and as dull as donkey's work. Masatoshi Matsukawa had struggled to evoke his usual bold and authoritative stance but instead offered the boy a coy reductive parade of himself as a boy. At twelve years of age, it had puzzled Chiyoko Matsukawa why a man of such stature had suddenly reduced himself to a mere humble mortal. He wondered how the men of Hontoni had control over his father's affairs and to what extent their powers could reach him. He thought of the summoning of a samurai, with his sword leather-bound and protected, and the possible damage this samurai could do to his father. This made him feel so nauseous that he consumed more nitrogen from the air than necessary.

Chiyoko Matsukawa woke a second time and witnessed the bombardment of bodies at a busy metro station. He stood in their midst, untouched by their chaos but feeding off the misery they conveyed. Their electricity had made him alert to his surroundings, and he became absorbed in the neon blue, white, pink and red of the Tokyo billboards, dripping with bad Japanese calligraphy. In the foreground, a platform of passengers waited, assured of the punctuality of the next Shinkansen train.

All clear! Chiyoko heard on the station's public address system. All clear! he heard again. It seemed that the public address system had been tampered with and was causing difficulties for its user. Then the message became faint and almost inaudible. I think we've lost this one, the voice said.

Chapter 28.

Harp Seal

Whatever are you doing here, Chiyoko? What are doing here? I asked you to give me your hand as these floors are bent and shaky. You seem to have taken too well to the dark, Matsukawa. It's as though you were kissing cousins with it.

Perhaps you could step outside of it, so I could see you better? Perhaps seeing your face would calm my nerves. Perhaps the benzodiazepine's had a field day with me, or perhaps I broke my limbs as I can't seem to move them. A hand here, Chiyoko, would you?

I had a dream about two domesticated seals, Christopher, two burly seals, one wanting to be stroked so desperately and the other wanting to be left alone while it enjoyed the routine of an afternoon nap beneath a coffee table. When I stroked the first seal, it wanted more. It craved my affection, Christopher, to the extent that it put me off and I withdrew myself from this seal.

When I approached the second harp seal to offer it a stroke of the same affection I had afforded the first, it lay there complacently and withdrew into a state of absolute nonchalance. When I came closer, it moved away further under the coffee table of no designated owner. I was unsure of where I was then, and I am unsure of where it happened now.

Christopher, the second seal moved away, showing clearly it didn't want to be bothered, Chiyoko said as he stood still as a pole and embraced the dark shade of night. Not by me or anyone else, he continued. When I reached out a third time, convinced it would indulge in my affection, it snarled at me with a gust of its frustration boiling over from the bottom of its balding belly. The threat was real, Christopher. It showed its teeth to me, Christopher. The message was clear enough: any further approach would be met with a bite that was likely to draw blood.

Fascinating, Chiyoko, said Christopher, but what has your dream got to do with why you are here? What are you doing here in my room, Chiyoko?

Christopher, the first seal jumped into my lap and gave me a great big slap across the face with its hind flippers, suggesting it accepted all the affection I had to offer. In spite of that, I was fool enough to offer kindness to the second seal.

Christopher, I found myself relenting towards the first seal. I was content with the needy seal and the position it had cornered me into, lying flappy in my lap and drooling with pleasure. Christopher, I also developed a sense of acceptance towards the second seal's apathy as it lay nonchalantly beneath the coffee table. I finally settled for the eager seal in my lap and its craving for my affection.

Chiyoko, I beg of you, what has your dream got to do with why you are here? asked Christopher. What are you doing here in my room, and why wouldn't you help me? I said these floors are shaky.

You ever wonder where you are, Christopher? You ever wonder whether I am perhaps just an illusion? Chiyoko added. Notice anything strange? I have, Chiyoko said. I'm not entirely sure about it, but I'm certain it isn't what you think it is, this place that you call your room.

You are talking crazy shit, Chiyoko. Which illusion are you referring to? A minute ago, I saw you playing a concerto solo; you were about twelve, and I was certain that was an illusion. Now I wake up and find you in my bedroom, hiding in the dark and telling tales of harp seals. You've gone crazy mad, Chiyoko Matsukawa.

I liked to think of it that way, too, that I was indeed going crazy, Christopher. I am just as bemused by it, said Chiyoko Matsukawa. As I say, I am unsure about it; I have no control over it. I am here in your room alright but am unsure of how I got here. Although it seems strangely natural to me, as though I had casually walked in on you having a dream. Again, I am unsure of whatever it is that is going on here, Christopher. I am unsure.

Christopher! Chiyoko Matsukawa called out. I am certain there is more to all this that we both are witnessing. Regarding my not helping you, I really want to but something innately holds me back. It's as though it wasn't my place to help you, as though I was meant to be here just watching you, watching you in whatever you were meant to be experiencing, Christopher, whatever you were meant to be doing before you saw me at the door, comfortable as the dark itself.

The two seals, Christopher, I think were a message to us both. We don't always get what we want, but we certainly get what we need. Perhaps that's it. Perhaps that's why I am here in your room, to tell you this, Christopher. Perhaps that's why my legs are as weighty as lead steel and why I can't seem to make myself move to help you. Perhaps that's why I am just as confused about these apparent illusions as they in fact appear natural to me, as I am sure they do to you, too. Perhaps we should both surrender in acceptance and allow ourselves to drool, like the first harp seal.

Chiyoko! Christopher called out into the empty space where his friend had been standing, resilient as when he had been in the midst of a busy Tokyo station and was being bombarded by a rage of human traffic.

Chapter 29.

Birth of a Harp Seal

The sounds of depressed rubber returned as the bothered Bombay lurked at dawn. Christopher pondered on what world he had been a part of. He listened intently, but none of it made sense, not even the piercing white light that broke intermittently through the veil of his lucid dreams.

With healthy presumption, a dose of alkaloid reasoning and a measured kick of scepticism, Christopher leaned towards the gravity of isoprene as that had been more consistent. The squeaks of rubber soles went about their business on a polished linoleum floor.

Christopher Myen witnessed the birth of a harp seal's first pup. He saw its wings at the time of its birth and how large they were compared to the rest of its body. They are usually flightless at birth, and any subsequent harp seal born from the same mother has no wings.

It puzzled him the amount of effort it took to birth a harp seal; he concluded it was equivalent to the effort of two able-bodied men. He watched the mother push and saw that grace was on her side, whilst hope lingered in the far distance below splinters of light. He waited for the newborn to breathe, assured that the possibility of failure was as real as gravity itself.

Once delivered, the offspring's heart beat with Darwinian rhythms and its mother craved a maternal bond. Myen noticed the strangeness of the newborn shrinking to the size his fist, and in the blink of an eye, its delicate fur receded and its wings reduced to small balls.

As the seasons went by, the first-born harp seal acquired siblings. All, of course, looked up to it, expecting miracles to be performed as it was the only harp seal with protruding limbs that resembled wings.

When it failed to perform the miracle of flight, as they had seen the fowls of the air do, graciously and without effort, they gave up hope and pitied the harp seal with bulbs for wings. They watched it plummet to the ground, and its tireless desperation became something of an enigma as they never harboured the desire to fly themselves or borne non-functional wings.

Myen witnessed many unsuccessful trials. He saw that a wish had nestled in the eyes of its siblings for the first-born to take flight and for it to teach them the joys of having wings and the feelings of being up in the air, so they cheered it on as it failed, they cheered it on as it buried its head in mud and ate of dirt, they cheered it on as its soul became a hollow shell of dark nothingness, until it hugged itself into a small ball and lurked in dark places of biblical intensity.

When success came as tiny specs breaking through a veil, Christopher Myen saw that a spark had been lit in the young seal's belly. A bolt had developed that channelled electricity through its nerves until the seal gathered enough courage to let itself fail and embrace the pain of falling. It pursued the act of flight and failed miserably over and over again until a muscle formed in its appendix and grew feathers of ambition that made its wings emerge like a new rhythm. When the gales were high, it harnessed their abundance and immersed itself in their generosity.

Christopher Myen counted, in the passing of two full weeks, a hundred falls to earth; he observed much gracious harnessing of the wind, a steady building of its wing muscles and a thickening of its feathers, as robust as resins of isoprene. When the harp seal achieved a degree of success through a lift sustained longer than a second, it kept at it until the sun went down. Then it kept at it until it sustained it for longer than a minute until its muscles could take no more.

The next morning, the harp seal was out in the open field. It wobbled through the dirt as harp seals do, then sprinted with its flappy feet as it had done the previous day, putting its non-functional wings to use until it took to the air. This was after months of agony and weeks of disappointment and days when little success was achieved and hours when perseverance had been its only companion, willing it on for minutes on end.

The first-born harp seal garnered all its might and all its courage until it, too, could soar through the skies as if it had never had to learn to fly, as it had never had to learn to run or crawl or use its flippers and had never buried its head in a pool of water and its eyes never got sore from mud-salt every time it failed and crashed to earth.

Its siblings watched on in amazement, having longed for the day when they would see their eldest take to the skies and fly over their heads, soaring through the clouds like the birds of the courtyards.

As time went by, and with little effort, each harp seal sibling became comfortable with the notion of wobbling on its hind flippers. They enjoyed the ease of the breeze that brushed against their chest and the pleasure of seeing above the horizon, as history had afforded them only a lower glimpse of the world they resided in and a strained neck from the constant wobble of their bellies in mud.

They thanked the first-born harp seal for showing courage, as if it were not for its tiresome pursuit of flight, they would be stuck to the ground, their bare chests rubbing against the earth and their necks sore from a constant stretching to gain a small glimpse of the great wide world before them.

Christopher Myen woke up to the provocation of O Kaori incense, a priest at hand's length, and Chiyoko Matsukawa at his Steinway & Sons piano, running rounds of chords and progressions beneath the evening moon.

Chapter 30.

Opium Heaven

As the old man danced himself to an early grave, the smell of hard liquor had seduced him into getting rid of a competing vice, his love for cheap whores, a habit he had long ago picked up as a young soldier in the Queen's army. Loitering through the bomb-ridden cobbled roads of a Central European town, a mischievous Slavic business man had stumbled upon an opportunity to make vast wealth from men so far from home. They had endured months of loneliness and had an insatiable desire for the musky smell, with a zesty tang, and the wetness of a woman.

A hit of opium had driven the old man mad for days. He was sweating profusely, his eyes were as wild as fire and his heart pounded like a lion's moments before it mauled its prey. Like a buffet, the naked flesh of a woman basked in the unsteady flicker of a broody red light. The old man had long forgotten his promises to the new church. I mean, if it had been good enough for George… he thought, weighing up the alkaloid chocolate as it sizzled on a spoon, poised to fight his demons.

This he knew well. His son had been of much a similar age to the boy when it had happened. Splattered red on the wall, the boy slumped into a pool of his own blood, the old man with a gun in his hand; he witnessed a younger version of himself in the mirror. These things can happen to anyone, he heard the man say to him. It was an accident, the man proclaimed. You cannot be too hard on yourself. Time has passed since the miscue, and it was written off, the younger man in the mirror professed. The gun jammed and misfired, that's what it says in the log, the young man in the mirror added.

The old man witnessed himself weak as a newborn suckling on his mother's bosom, wet as the day he was born and new to the world. I killed him, the old man said. I killed that little boy, he shouted. I shot that boy and now he is dead cold to the world, the old man cried.

When the heat of the night had woken the old man in a cold sweat, he had reached for the bottle and drowned himself with a slug of booze. We were at war, he said. The enemy was at bay, and how was I supposed to know that the quiet rattle was that of a boy and not a militant? He continued to cry until the moon showed its face from within the clouds and the air was as thin as a sheet of ice. I'll suffer if it's for the rest of my life. The flesh of women doesn't satisfy me, and the hit of hot boiled opium simmers but for a few sparse moments, and time of the magnitude of thirty years only brushes away at me and leaves me with increased potency, my own son a man with a daughter of his own, yet the boy haunts me, he lamented. I'll do good with these few years of mine, and if it's the last thing I do, these smouldering eyes of an abandoned youth I'll make mine. Yes, he'll fight me over it; he'll fight me. He did say, in my old age, how was I supposed to fend for a little orphan boy? Yes, he'll fight me for it; he'll fight with the same bothered spirit of his mother, knowing very well I'm addicted to the pain. Boy…. these opium wonders have got me in a bother.

Christopher Myen witnessed the old man fall to the floor and curl into a ball, clasping his bottle against his abdomen. He heard him jibbering about least favoured fortunes. Every man suffers, he finally said when he noticed the voyeur of Christopher Myen standing in the shadows to the continuum of the stream of light from a TV set. Every man suffers, the old man repeated to the presence of Christopher Myen, I suppose regardless of creed or stance. His eyes were fixated on the image of Christopher occupying the shadows. They do, even if it's quietly, he quavered and embraced his bottle against his abdomen with even more care than he had done before. He rose to his feet in an instant and held onto an image of Christopher Myen. He pulled him into the limelight emitted by the TV set, releasing a chuckle that was more about his ability to bring a sense of reality to the scene than the bemusement of a startled Christopher Myen.

Christopher opened his eyes and saw that he was standing before two large canvasses hanging in the atrium. He remembered them from the time he was ten years of age when he had helped to paint them. The old man gazed emptily into his own creation, lost in the moment; he stared dead into the colours of his swirls and deemed them circular nothingness. Chasing passion, the old man blurted out and chuckled to himself with his bottle of rum clasped against his chest. The faintest of ideas simply ran away with him as he stood and took in his own creation. Chasing passion, he repeated and turned to face Christopher. He started to recite the numbers 4…2…1…2…6 over and over. I hope it doesn't consume me, he said. He released an alcoholic burp that reeked of ammonia and only found his footing after he'd taken another sip of his rum. And leave me with nothing, he concluded.

When Christopher realised he might be in one of his other dreams, he walked towards the table where a paint brush was perched on a pot, and he acquainted himself with the scattered possessions of the old man. He read aloud to himself in his mind *OPOS RA42126 F Wilson* on a dog tag splattered with paint residue that gave it a mustard yellow hue.

Whatever do you mean, old man? Christopher Myen finally said. Old man… why did you draw these circles? he asked.

Son… to rid me of my desires as they are burning, blurted out the old man.

Chapter 31.

Crash

On that night, waves of auburn burnt into the clouds. It was also the night of the crash. A marriage of words occurred and an exchange of liquid thoughts penetrated his subconscious. Christopher Myen lay there and watched the fall of debris – plastics and steel and minerals and ores and rubbers of all sorts.

The night of the crash had been a night of many revelations of starved wonders, bludgeoned courses, troubled attachments and lost ambitions.

It was a night of chased euphoria, of beautiful whispers, of flesh-selling facades and of dark lies and wonderful perspirations, a night of measured delusions and careful jeopardy. The woman had appeared to him, as cold as the wintry night and as spiced as an old rose in a vase of aged lavender water.

It was a night when Christopher became uncomfortable with the idea of comfort itself and rejected its offerings as fleeting pleasure. He lay there watching an O Kaori burn, a good burn, and Fleur Dominica's exertions falling dumb and as wise as the old man's dancing himself to a dose of alkaloid reasoning.

On impact, things became much clearer to Christopher Myen. He recounted moments of his own birth as though he were reliving the very moments, breathing in a fraction of oxygen so that it filled his lungs, and in high hopes of capturing revelations of floating shadows, the ones that didn't mimic but danced around his bedpost and onto his clothing where they hung.

In the mouldy cracks in the wall, fungi thrived and multiplied in an asexual process. Christopher Myen witnessed the thoroughbreds chewing leftover straw in the yard, their dung as pungent as sugary fermentation, and a wish hung over their heads like a cloud for him to bath in their dung and wash himself black.

Myen witnessed the passing of faces, of Chiyoko Matsukawa at his Steinway & Sons conjuring up Japanese myths; Ayer Frederickson at his gran cassa, beating into the leather as though a spirit was lost within its rims and the assault on the leather was an attempt to release it; Sebastian Evans holding his Ibanez like a missed love and his sudden realisation that nothing would ever be enough for him but to reach the wavering summits of undetermined adorations. He witnessed Fleur Dominica as red as the burning bush of alatus, pleading for him to consult with her oneirologist, Tamide Quieros, as his dreams had become too big for her and as overbearing as taxes. She traded with him her darkest moments, ones she saw in her dreams, and shared her most intimate illusions, such as when she was a little girl and the passing of her Aunt Dupe. A bisque doll she was given she named after her aunt, with red weaves for hair like an alatus plant, and all this before the month that she bled.

The night of the crash had been a night of companionship with his piccolo Bb in hand. It blared a rusty note that was more out of tune than the Bombay's shriek and lacked truth, yellow as the brass and as gold as rawness itself. The balloons of his mouth struggled to bring his instrument to life; he watched his music suffer a fall of seventy percent of cast copper and the rescue of his body from a hierarchy in which his needs had become secondary, and he drifted like lethargy between sheets of lucid dreams.

He witnessed his body become a rag doll of shifted decisions sine qua non. His head slumped onto his chest and the fall of rain glass made little incisions in his skin, drawing his blood in tiny scattered specks that looked more like treasured litmus. Their variant revealed a hue of depleted water, high in salt, high in benzodiazepines and reeking of diffused carbon dioxide.

The porcelains were in unison, white as overalls, and held smiles of foreverness on their faces, plain as river landscapes and as contoured as banks of river bends. Their names instantly filled his head like a sponge: Ms Benevolent and Dr St Patrick. Myen overheard their conversation in scared voices, debating potions of healing, and sensed a thirst for mad passion burning in the loins of one of them.

We're fully depleted at 8:45, he heard.

AM, to be precise.

I concur, he heard the first voice say.

He is stable again. We almost lost him, he heard the second voice say. His shakes are gone.

Then good, said the first voice.

Isotonic on order, IFR? questioned the second.

I concur.

It's a1000 max on the bag, millilitres by the patch, concur?

I concur, said the first voice.

I say we have at least 600 minutes – that's 10 hours, replied the second voice. Yes, 10, said the first voice. Concur?

I concur, replied the second.

Ten hours to match the beat it is then, said the first voice.

Chapter 32.
Porcelain

Christopher Myen could tell in an instant what time of day it was from the freshness of the air that drifted into his room. He could tell with a degree of precision the measure of day it was going to be from the sort of mood that came along with the warmth of sun burning on his skin and the quality of light that strayed into the room where he found his body.

One porcelain turned into flesh and kissed the other on the cheek, leaving a cold imprint of saliva where her lips had been. The mucus dissipated into a mist and left the face of stone with a print. The human one held the chin of the porcelain, examined it for life and saw a gaze she knew too well, one of emptiness like a stroll in the dark into an empty room where even echoes were lost and the pitch dark lingered on like good hopes and good deeds and misplaced kindness.

Patricia Benevolent rubbed the head of Myen and placed a damp cloth on his head. She checked his temperature and recounted with precision the number of beads on her black topaz necklace. They weren't truly black but, in the light, a mosaic of multiple hues of dark grey, light blue, dim silver, emerald green and a small hint of vermillion orange, the same as those on the floors of the house where one Christina DeSilva had lived.

Patricia traced her index finger over the cracks and measured the width of the face of the porcelain. She made a quiet wish for the porcelain man to come alive, a wish that only a small fraction of her breath would be what it took to bring the stone to life, as though it were rich in oxygen with a whiff of nitrogen.

Myen struggled with these versions of his lucid dreams, a stone man being consecrated by a woman, as he saw it. St Patrick, she mumbled quietly into the chest of stone. She pressed her head against its breast, in something that looked like a search. When she failed to find a heartbeat, she whispered the name of one Dr Kenneth St. Patrick and, making her ear a stethoscope, placed it repeatedly against its chest.

A cold imprint was planted on Myen's chest. He could hear the beatings of his own heart, pounding away like water boiling in a pot. He saw the necklace and witnessed her compulsive fingering, as though she were making a confession, working the beads like a rosary. When she was finished, she stood up and went towards the window sill. She took in the brilliance of the sun, wiped her lips of excess Kaolin and rid herself of any alkaline laced in the dust. She lit herself a cigarette and smoked till the sun went down.

In the evening, when the sun finally disappeared behind

the thick clouds that held the skies to ransom, she walked towards the body of Christopher Myen and recited the numbers 4, 2, 1, 2, 6. She repeated them as though to summon him from a deep sleep. She gave her Rubicon scarf a rub and adjusted it to the left, letting the cool breeze onto her neck to ease her stress. Then she whispered the numbers 4, 2, 1, 2, 6 into his ear again, as though his mind were a safe and the numbers a code to unlock him from a deep sleep.

When she failed to rouse him, she turned to the porcelain and said, I think he is as good as gone, dead to the world, and all that's left of him is the physical.

There is no point to all this rhetoric – he's simply gone, said Ms Benovelence.

Dead as stone, just as you are, she said.

Christopher Myen ransacked his higher faculty for an explanation of what he had seen. He debated the dose he had taken, possibly one too many, he thought, one too many that plunged me into an abyss of punctured dreams. I've come alive and yet find myself simmering in them, boiling away like water in a pot on a stove in a kitchen.

Myen recalled the last time he had seen Fleur Dominica. It had been a month and two days, according to his reckoning. He measured days by the angle of the sun and by the caws of the crows that he heard from the side yard, early in the mornings, and by the freshness of horse dung that drifted into his room. He recalled with strict accuracy their conversation beneath the stray beams of fledging light, when the most bizarre had been a comfort and shared between the two of them.

When Fleur Dominica had struggled to speak, Myen had concluded that she was nearing mania. She had battled to remember the most basic facts, such as her name, or recognise the very place where they were sitting, beneath the dull light.

When he tried to move his limbs and they wouldn't respond, he started to question why he couldn't leave his room or snap out of his lucid dreams. Why couldn't he just get up, walk out the door and enjoy even the irritating creak of the worm-eaten stairway leading down from his bedroom?

Myen shifted his attention to the lines of blood laced on the floor of his bedroom. He could smell the heaviness of sodium and chloride and knew it was the blood from a horse. He wondered where it had come from, why it had been there, and what had caused the death of a horse in his room. Such beauty, the waste of a thoroughbred, its blood scattered like red geranium petals on his floor. When he failed to comprehend the dead horse's fate, he surrendered himself to the notion that all had been a dream and none of it had any bearing on reality.

Chapter 33.

Euphoria

Christopher Myen witnessed the strain of pain on the face of Christina DeSilva. She was sitting with her hands in her hair, running a loop through them as though they were electrical cords, concocting renditions of electricity.

Myen considered the body of DeSilva to be not as appealing or appeasing in its full nudity. He recalled his first draw of 5-MeO-dimethyltryptamine like his first love, lost in pursuit of lust. He concluded ultimately that the discreetness of flesh was much more alluring than the full spread of a woman's form. He witnessed her rational spirit dance and the look of pampered hurt on her face, her undulations like geometry and the way she wore her expressions like a mask, displaying them like trophies of utter euphoria, tugging on the rush like a train going through a tunnel and her wails like prayers to a cosmic deity.

Later that evening, Christopher Myen witnessed the old man in the distance, dancing his dance of drunken outcries and nonsensical chants about the sun and a time soon to come. He moved in circles and pruned them as though to reduce their turbulence, dampening his steps whenever the draw of alcohol wore off, until he gathered enough courage to drown himself with yet another gulp. Then he continued spewing his latent absurdity and reciting the numbers 42126, 42126, with barely a hint of his lisp: four, two, one, two, sicth. He nursed his jittery performance with the warmth of reminiscence and brochures of war memories, the sight of his trigger and the blood of men it had spilled, replacing their dogmas with a shimmering existence that was felt but unseen.

When the sway of his liquor subsided, he slumped to the ground, moaning endlessly about the numbers. They will be the end of me, he groaned and dug at the wood, etching the numbers irritably into the floor with his fingers.

Christopher woke to find the old man had gone, leaving the numbers etched into the wood like a call to action inked in the red of his blood. When he tried to get up and walk, he fell to the ground and smelt the salt from the old man's blood in the same spot where the thoroughbred had shed its blood. Kamari licked the blood of the old man, winced to get rid of the excess and meowed for attention. It seemed to tug on Christopher from the depths of his sleep and bring him to a place he knew too well, his bedroom, where the fungal growth had matured and gave off tiny spores that he inhaled and which caused a difficulty in his chest, colonising it with a red rash. The cracks in the walls signified that his loft was old and in need of repairs and was slowly edging towards a collapse.

Why is it you cannot walk? Kamari asked, lying on the TV set with its tail swirling in the air. You can't be bedridden at such a young age?

Christopher tried his arms and found that he could not move them; he tried his legs and found them to be heavy as lead. And what a wonder it is that I find myself talking to a Bombay and it drinks of the blood of a vanished man! Christopher said.

Well, the world is full of wonders, and if you would only let yourself be so vulnerable, you would know that yourself, Kamari replied.

And what would you know of being vulnerable, Kamari? asked Christopher. You're only a feline with the simplest of needs and the basest of instincts, so ingrained that you need not make yourself think your whole life, he spat.

So you think it's simple to be a feline? Kamari asked. I lick myself so tirelessly clean I could choke on my own hairballs.

If you were to fall to the ground this very moment, you would still land on all fours, wouldn't you? asked Christopher.

Yes, and if I were to ask you to imagine the moon with half its face covered in cream, you would, at a moment's notice, wouldn't you? Kamari retorted, rubbing its back against the radiator to get rid of the scent of old rose in the room.

You speak with a lens of single scope, Christopher, implying that I could be written off with no ceremony to mourn my existence; wouldn't you call that being vulnerable?

Kamari quizzed, sitting beneath the dull light of the moon and rubbing its nose with its paw.

I say parallels; all is parallels. If you bother to look beyond forms, you'll see what it is exactly that haunts you when you sleep, Christopher, from the woman that dances with the spirits above your torso and the voyeurs of shadows that watch you, to a porcelain couple that mimic an existence, stealing you away into drifted illusions. You wonder how a woman's form could be so weaponised, yet you bask in euphoria, with eyes in the clouds travelling a million miles and chasing the passion of your past life. When you fail, you let the pain consume you, rendering yourself paralysed. You ever heard the sounds of a trumpet no longer in use, dust in its pipes and embouchure out of tune?

Kamari leapt onto the bed of Christopher Myen and continued in its felinities of licking its paws and rubbing its nose with saliva. Well, you might just be the same as that old dusty trumpet, out of tune and out of play. Unless you wake up to euphoria and wash away your setbacks, they'll consume you.'

Chapter 34.

Mirrored Isomer

Of the voices that taunted Christopher Myen deep in his sleep, palpitating in his subconscious like boiling water, he heard the voice of St Patrick.

An eye on the pulse, Myen heard the voice say. Keep the drip flowing.

Pupils are constricted, no large mass, uttered another voice with urgency.

No large mass obstructing? questioned Dr Kenneth St Patrick.

Yes, I concur, the female voice said. Then he sensed both voices dissipating like the wind. In their place was a sharp light that stunned for a moment until it, too, dissipated like the wind.

Myen witnessed himself in the perils of inertia and concluded that he might, in fact, be dead and existing in another world. He recognised a single name that had anchored him to the side of the living, Patricia Benevolent, the porcelain beau with topaz necklace of varying hues and a silk Rubicon scarf. She recounted her moments of loneliness to him in the quiet vacancy of closed eyes and whispered how lucky he had been, leaving a crackle that lasted as long as a quarter of a fourth of a minute until it also dissipated like the wind.

Myen felt the cold impression of a kiss on his forehead. The scent of fired clay whizzed past and the freshness of new blossoms on a Prunus mume lingered in the air, long after her quiet exit from the room. He heard the calls of a Bonin fox far in the distance and felt the hardening in his loins.

He recalled her promises, the ones he knew she could never keep as they were too difficult a task for any one soul to attempt, her calls for his liberation from the depth of her belly and the straining for wisdom as she built up his lust, the feral entertainment she gave it, in the quiet refuge of humble nights.

Christopher Myen witnessed himself being washed away by yet another of his lucid dreams, carried away by a wind of delirious visions and finding himself in new places, discarded into them as hurricane droppings of uprooted property.

When he woke, he witnessed Christina DeSilva in conversation with her mother. She asked how bad the flu was and whether or not she'd recover. She was lying amongst goose down pillows and buried her head in their warmth, hoping for a day when she could once again be out in the fields and run after the birds, chase Christopher into the mud and listen out for him as he counted numbers downwards from 10. He heard Christina's mother reassure her daughter that she'd get better soon; the lentil soup remedy she'd made would have her springing about the place in no time. You will be out chasing that boy from down the road in no time, you will be, she said. You will be able to play hide and seek again with that boy, what's his name? she asked.

Christopher, is it? suggested the girl's father.

Yes, that's it – Christopher, then both voices dissipated like mist in his head.

He heard the movements of rubber on linoleum floors and the clanging of utensils far in the distance. He continued to pine for the visions of Christina DeSilva ill in her bed as he concluded a clue might be locked in them. He might gain an understanding of himself, why it was he remained paralysed and was haunted by long-gone voices in his head, why it was a woman spirit danced above his torso every fortnight and left behind a scent of old rose in a vase of aged lavender water, his sleep walk to the rest room where a blemished mirror hung and his fruitless practices on his piccolo Bb, blowing into the embouchure a thrust of air that was empty of a draw of something surreptitious and addictive.

When Patricia Benevolent returned to find him in a state of unrest, she called St Patrick. He seems to be coming back to us, she said into the phone's receiver. His pupils are uneven, one's bigger than the other; they are like Ebbinghaus's balls of illusion, and I think he might be crying, too. Yes, crying, she repeated into the receiver. Is this normal? I mean he's been half dead for almost eight months and now he cries? This can't be normal, can it? I mean what should I do? she asked. His eyes are still, I mean they don't move, yet they pour out tears uncontrollably. What should I do? she asked a distant St Patrick. A muffled version of his voice seeped through the phone's earpiece. Re-enacting, you say? Patricia waited for his reply. Yes, I know, she said. Perhaps I should put a mirror to his face and let it catch the light in his eyes? Yes, yes, a mirror, she said. Yes, like moving mirrors, perhaps like a plant would chase it to catch the light, she muttered. Yes… his response to light. Could it be that he is dreaming and this unsettles him? she asked, waiting for a muffle and a cough. When St Patrick's voice finally came through the receiver, it was serene. We broker him some help, you say, and give him a gentle nudge? she repeated into the receiver. As much as we can give him? Well… if that's what you say, then I'll do just that.

When Myen woke, he found himself the worse for wear, facing a wall and a window, with the clamour of a pitta bird in the air.

Chapter 35.

A Good Cry

Christopher Myen heard the muffled pulse of a metronome tick, the gentle quiet of early morning, then the clamour of voices that seemed to be in a foreign language that grew louder in his head. Hela, hela, hela hey! he heard.

He heard the screech of a train coming to an abrupt stop, the buzz of electricity, an ad occupying a screen with the face of a man overly expressive peddling commodity stocks, and the scrambling of telephone lines and internet connectivity that went on longer than twenty minutes. (By his calculations, it might well have been for a century.) He heard the continuous running of trains on a line, voices talking in a documentary, the swish of gears changing, and the crank of an automotive. Then he had a sudden feeling of being tremendously alive, a marvellous moment of being on a sunny beach with sun-baked bodies, the sort of place where beautiful people go to make beautiful memories, and he heard the breaking of seashells from a fishing net in preparation for the next voyage.

Myen heard another voice enter his head. All of life is a stage, and you need not care so much, he heard the Bombay say. A platform for us to play, to parade, to protrude, and to prance around like fools, I say. You think I am so serious, yet I am on my last roll of the dice. Squandered all, I say; squandered eight of them on frivolous thrills, if you're asking – but only if you're asking. Now, let's see what's getting you so down that you take it so seriously? What bothers you so much? Myen observed the Bombay leap from an upper shelf onto a cupboard next to it, curl up its tail in a swirl and then jump back onto the floor where it gingerly walked in two loops around Christopher's leg. It brushed its tail against him so its presence could be felt, then it leaped onto the bed where Myen sat and watched the early morning sun burning its plasma.

I'll be poised with clarity on the meaning of it all, said Kamari. You see, it's like picking at broken crumbs of a pie and wanting more of it whole, and I get so hungry for more of the delicious pie, if you follow? I'll tell you a little secret, said Kamari, as it walked the window ledge facing Myen, its tail in the air and almost a smile on its face. What if I told you that your life is a play and that you are only acting it out as well as you are meant to do, from the visuals? You're so primed only so you can role play them into the elements. Everyone's life is like that, all taking cues predestined, and isn't that so funny? said Kamari, the presumption of a grin resting comfortably on its face. We fool ourselves into thinking we're so clever, so ultimate in our being, and we initiate our choices as though they were our very own. We've chosen them, we say, when we're merely walking through them like a grid, said Kamari and rubbed its head against the wood of one leg of the bed frame. We yearn so much for originality. I mean we're really just a copy of something else, said the Bombay, as it licked on a hernia, released itself from a stretch and collapsed into yet another pose. Perhaps you accept it all and fall for grace, said Kamari, and it becomes clearer to you. Do you ever wonder about the concept of time travel? I mean if we go fast enough east, we could find ourselves in the future; likewise, if we go fast enough west, we could end up in the past or something of sort. It's just a thought that bothers me, if you follow my drift? What's the rush in living life so fast, anyways? it asked a desolate Christopher Myen. I myself prefer the solitude and savour moments at slower pace, if you follow my drift? That's where the real magic happens – in the slows.

If you find yourself not wanting, then you've indeed freed yourself from it all. Kamari gave a good yawn and collapsed into yet another stretch by the side of Myen. From the shadow voyeurs to the movement of porcelain and their voices, to the old man, the gypsy and the shaman, the mustard paint of circles and numbers four, two, one, two, six, my advice – if, of course, you're asking me – is to check out of the business of love as you're very bad at it.

The sun shifted further west into a cloudless sky. By his account, Myen had spent the whole day sitting on his bed, without so much as going to the restroom or craving food.

Before long, he fell back into bed, from which he awoke and heard the voice of Christina DeSilva. So sorry I made you mine. I feel that I held onto you for too long. The beginning of something that felt like a tear began to form on Christopher Myen's face.

Chapter 36.
A Good Purge

When the TV set regained its signal, it was to an image of the famous concert pianist, Chiyoko Matsukawa, flashed upon the concave screen. It showed off the purity of his white lapels against the backdrop of stage light and in contrast with the sharps and flats of his Steinway & Sons. His head was buried low so his face was in shadow, and the only thing that made him appear human was his nose caught by the light and the base of his chin that protruded from the shadow like an iceberg jutting out of the water.

Christopher heard the fingers of Chiyoko Matsukawa make a sombre start on a minor chord. He heard the run of his fingers on the keys like the trickle of honey. The image of harp seals appeared to him, forty-two in an orchestra of two bassoons, two oboes, two clarinets, two horns, two trumpets and two flutes. A blue and green light flashed on cue, and twelve of the harp seals pulled out violins and placed them gently over their left shoulders; a further six joined in with cellos rested endpins to the ground; then twelve more harp seals pulled out violas and replicated the actions of the first twelve harp seals. A timpanist harp seal wobbled onto the stage and, as though late in its obligations, made briskly for its instrument. It offered a nod of apology to the conductor that held a baton in its flipper and waved it as though ready to conduct.

A short moment passed, and the music began with the chords of the violins' gentle serenade; their bows against the strings whetted the appetite for the music that was about to take form. The clarinets followed suit, playing the legendary Beethoven's Concerto No 3 Allegro Con Brio. Chiyoko sat still, with his head above the keys of his Steinway & Sons, in a trance about the marvelousness of music, its grand gestures and its contribution to a civilised existence. When he finally started to play, it was with an ascending scale, with his fingers waltzing over the notes until he finally collapsed onto the very keys that had inspired him.

The notion of flight came to Christopher in his bed as he listened to the music aired on the TV, and many conflicts of interest circled around in his head like water. He mused on water's gift of transcendence and its many states, to its eventual incarnation as an ephemeral mist. When the Bombay came to him, it was to say that the liquid purge of its feline mind had compelled it to share the things that had bothered it. Feline it may be, but it had suffered the same fate as its owner of falling asleep at every inopportune hour of the day, to awake to a reoccurrence of nonsensical existence. The Bombay circled the bed post, then settled into a ball at the base of the bed. It recounted its regrets of not having truly loved anyone except itself and then it passed out. When it awoke again, it was to recount yet another of its regrets, that of not truly following its heart and chasing birds at dawn; it had rather settled for the comfort of well-selected wet food served on flat dishes. It passed out again until the ninth hour and awoke to say it hadn't gathered quite enough courage to change its course; if it had done so, it would have chosen the setting of a well-curated cat cafe where it would have made an art of being the most well-loved and cared-for cat in the place, but this in itself, it noted, was yet another of its selfish, deluded ambitions. Whichever way it panned out, it admitted, it was ever fated to be the most selfish Burmese house-dwelling cat at heart.

The TV set regained its signal and a re-run of the popular cult series *Sueños* came on, with Fleur Dominica mid-way in conversation with her oneirologist. Tamide Queiros was questioning her about her temperament and her attitude to love.

Have you ever loved anyone other than yourself? she asked.

I can't imagine not ever being loved, Dominica replied, with only the slightest of interest in the subject presented to her. It is the quintessential reason I exist – to be loved, she added and feinted into her usual tactic of diverting attention away from the subject of love. Queiros asked her what she thought it might mean to suffer.

To suffer? she said. Well, if they suffer, it will only be because of my love for them. He or she should count themselves lucky.

Tamide Queiros scribbled the word *insostenible* on her pad, legibly enough for the viewers to read it. She bit on the end of her pen and weighed up her thoughts, like two sides of a coin, about the luscious body of Fleur Dominica as she had become something of a spectacle in her mind: her furloughed presence on the screen and resting on a chaise longue beneath dim lights that offered more than a suggested premise for seduction. There she was spirited away as she always was in the late afternoons.

The TV proceeded to broadcast a North Atlantic edition of National Geographic about harp seals in the Artic. The young pups suckled on their mothers, and their milky white fur was astounding to see on the screen. The mother harp seal was teaching her young pup to swim, her maternal instinct expressed in protracted, anxious cooing. In the end, she uttered tonal honks and grunts of delight when her young pup dived beneath the ice, confirming that it had been designed to take to the water.

The purge, the Bombay said, is that your problem isn't your problem at all but rather what others project onto you. If you are alive and breathing, then it seems there is hope.

Chapter 37.

The Chronicle of a Shaman

In the throes of a North Indian hallucinogen, he travelled into cosmic realms. The vivid colours of wild ornaments held to ransom any eyes that laid siege; gusts of wind blew tobacco smoke onto his face; a chant of the Inca, a dance to request presence, a hop on one foot, the measured breaks of shackles around his ankles and a call for guidance into a realm, a calling for something of a vision. There was also the patience of a mother's gentle wait, her voice in his ears at the break of dawn of reassurance that all was as it was meant to be and that the fight was a dumb man's game.

A cause for concern and a blessing of stillness were laced within his palms. The sweats of a long-gone time, a lifetime of stress, weighed on his mind, a dreamless existence in a mirror where he stood watching an isomer of himself at the tender age of ten, battling with his basic insecurities. In the end, this isomer of ten stood facing the mirror with two fists in the air and sought a challenge with a grown version of himself, and this dreamless existence faded away into a mist.

There was music in the air from a needle on a vinyl 45, the

sounds of one Miles Dewey Davis. In the notes of his trumpet, he witnessed solfeggio frequencies that floated about the space of his room in the melodies of Generique. A long while and a moment combined into a single note in his head and the face of DeSilva, with her fragrance of old rose in a vase of aged lavender water. She appeared to him as an aid, an elf-like being, and danced her ritual over his torso. When it came time for him to implode, it was to an eruption of wild colours from his groin. The shaman had a peculiar way of chasing off the damned from his sleeping body, sensing his resistance and blowing tobacco smoke onto his torso. A little while went by that he spent contented with a trivial kaleidoscope that had been both an oasis and a source of his anxieties. When he failed to make a success of his own death, he witnessed the rapid beating of a fan of dried leaves over his head, the smell of yeast and the familiarity of water on his tongue.

However odd these first experiences, he had mapped out the entirety of his odyssey, seeing himself outside of his ego, which had been something of a problem that needed to be put to bed. He smelt the drift of horse dung, which he associated with the early morning, from a stable a mile away from his apartment. The Bombay had its habit of coming into his room after dawn with a squirrel's dedication to cleansing, ridding his room of the late night's fragrance and replacing it with a little of its own scent as it was more comfortable with its urine in the air.

The Bombay collapsed into a stretch with its hernia exposed and its tail in a swirl. It's the simple things in life, the Bombay finally said. You can put on a good show, but in the end, it only makes you a good fool. You cannot fool the spirit; the spirit knows what it's doing. It's like two sides of the same thing. Have you ever witnessed two bulls going at it for no reason? the Bombay said. It would be a pointless exercise, don't you think?

The Bombay walked around the head of Christopher, fast asleep in a world of liquid neurons and a bulge of synapses, with the imitations of pitta birds, cobras and a snake charmer in the face of the woman and an invite as slight as a wave of her palm into a window of colours that was no more three-dimensional than the reality he had known with all of his five senses alive and overworked. The Bombay collapsed into yet another of its poses, lying on its belly so that its most intimate parts were seconds away from his nose. I will need you to hate me first before you can learn to love me; it is the only way you can learn to love me. Well, of course, if what you seek is to love me – I mean truly love me.

The shaman's shackles were back like a summer night's heat, his fan over his head and the presence of dried leaves dampening from the hit of an aliquot of N, N-D-methyltryptamine in a brew. Every second he awoke, it was to a vision of the old man and his dance in a circle. For two is for one to seek, the old man said. For two people is for one person to seek, the old man repeated. Two heads are always better than one, he said, chuckling at the notion that he had come up with the idea as though it had grown too heavy on his tongue and had simply fallen off into existence. Two heads are always better, he finally said.

Chapter 38.

The Chronicle of a Gypsy

Amid the revving of engines, the changing of motor gears and chains meshing with sprockets, a commuter sat on a bus with a lost look in his eyes and measured assurance of finding a gem at whatever destination he happened to find himself, although the loss of collagen from his skin and his fine wrinkles told tales of a thousandth let-down.

When the gypsy, Dupe Felicity, appeared to him, she told him that the hurricane had passed and there was no longer a need for him to worry. The worst of it is over, young-faced man, the gypsy said. We've come out the other end unscathed, and, indeed, you've done a brilliant job of it! You made a brilliant choice of a single dose, she said. I would have picked exactly the same kind. Her eyes were still behind shades that hid three-quarters of her face, and a lingering smirk said more about her indulgence in the vice of patience than it did of her pleasantries in matters of the heart.

I see no reason why she should bother you now, and perhaps I make myself a lot clearer. I am sure she no longer bothers you, and how long has it been since you've had yourself a good night's sleep? she asked. When he finally spoke, it was to say that he felt as though he had, indeed, lived a thousand existences but only one true life; all of the existences were fated to have the same sort of nonsensical feeling of an ending. So it bothers you to make sense of it all? the gypsy asked. The answer to the very question you ask stares you in the eyes, if only you could bring yourself to open them, she said, but your eyes are closed.

My eyes are open, Christopher said, open enough to see the day and that dusk is upon us and that electric moon is holding the skies to ransom out there as if painted on a canvass. I hear my heart beating, he said. It beats in cadence with the drumming of Ayer Frederickson, and all of my senses are alive and in sync with the numbers, the numbers he repeated in a gibber of 42, 12, 06 on a screen, he said. FC 42, SPO2 12 and RR 06 – these numbers he repeated. I see them presented to me on a screen and feel the presence of Ayer Frederickson beating on his drums. I feel his fingers on my chest and on my arm, searching for something. I feel them on my thigh, reaching for something, and the air electric and the taste of metal on my tongue.

The heart-rate monitor took readings of the variables. It captured Christopher's heart rate in cardiac frequency and the amount of oxygen in his blood in oxygen saturation and the rate at which he was breathing; the screen displayed it all in the rhythm of the highs and lows of his dreams. A clip on his finger took readings from the light it emitted. There were patches on his chest with wires that protruded with pinned electrodes and a display that said more of his state of mind than it did of his body; his dreams were charted and a lead pen depicted the vagaries of his hallucinations. When I wake, Christopher said, I find myself in the same spot as I have time and again, with my only gain the notion that time itself is my only true resource. There I find myself sitting in the afternoons as calm as the Bombay when it takes its nap, and all of it is a mere distraction from the fact that my vices got the better of me.

And are you so sure that I, too, am not gently pining for your attention? the gypsy said. With three quarters of my vision gone and taking my walks at the pace of a turtle, I, too, might want to have the best of you to myself. Why do you put so much weight on a woman that you hardly know? I'd say trust is another currency for you to consider. Can you trust that all that you see is real, that the blue of the sky is actually blue? asked the gypsy.

With the potency of her words on his mind and his conviction a concoction in a pot on a stove, boiling away into a mist, Christopher reprised his notion of falling cats at dawn. The way he saw it, it could only ever be remised as a daydream and as easy as water, its ever-changing form only ever coming back to being the same old thing: water. The gypsy Dupe Felicity hinted that all this nonsense was but a gentle cry from within, a primal yearning for something he wished to hold in his hands, a groaning, a coating of vernix and the ultimate wail of a newborn.

Chapter 39.

The Chronicle of a Soap Opera

When the TV set regained its signal, it was to a showing of the Japanese cult series *Otemae Chakai*. In a far drift from any sort of reality, it depicted an 18th-century minka house, in which a tokonoma displayed a scroll hanging from a bamboo rod with the saying that nothing was more benevolent than the sun peeking over the horizon at sunrise. From a floor of tatami, stepping stones led to a tranquil space and a conversation between Yamamoto Kasuga and Yamatoshi Ito, sitting quietly in the morning brewing matcha tea.

Isn't it funny, he said, that we can wake up in the morning to the feeling of being born anew and that the previous day seems but a dream? Yamatoshi Ito poured two cups of the brewed tea that steamed out of the bowls and the aroma of fresh leaves filled the room. Yes, Ito replied subtly. She wiped a ceramic bowl with precise dedication to the art, placed the hemp cloth in the slit in her kimono and presented two sweets on the dish. She wiped the sides of the dish with the same dexterity as she had done before and returned the cloth to the sides of her ribs, tucked beneath a gold and red patterned obi.

She lifted herself off the floor and tucked her feet beneath her torso.

Yes, she said in a bid to recapture his train of thought and continue the discussion, but all of it is merely an opinion, she finally said. She placed the dipper of a long ladle into the pot of boiling water and went through the ritual of agitating the finely milled matcha. We realise we've woken up into a trap of just being in another day, she said.

The quiet desperation of a soul, Kasuga added.

Wakatteru, precisely, uttered Ito with a hint of quiet satisfaction that her words had made an impression on him. She placed the bowl carefully in front of him and offered a courteous bow, which he returned.

When he drank his second serving, it was to show his appreciation that the matcha had indeed relieved him of any lingering stress; his sleep had relaxed him, and with his demons at bay, he savoured the moment.

When the hours of creativity pass, he said, we must look to another day. It is by this very notion that we must live; anything else results in misery.

Wakatta, replied Ito with a bow of respect to show that his words carried weight with her. How is it that we can spend a whole life time chasing a dream only to realise that it wasn't a dream but a nightmare? she asked.

That, too, replied Kasuga, is an opinion. It is a question of how things are perceived. The prey and the predator are one and the same thing: one cannot exist without the other. And which do you think is truly free – the prey or the predator?

Naturally… said Ito, I'd say the beast; the beast is free.

Wakatta, replied Kasuga and decided to drink another bowl of the brew. When he had finished his draught of finely milled matcha, he placed the bowl gently before him with the same dexterity as when he had picked it up.

The beast cannot be free, he eventually said. The beast is heavily dependent on its prey; if the prey ceases to exist, so does the beast.

So then, which is truly free? questioned Ito. The prey ceases to exist once eaten by the beast.

Wakatta, replied Kusaga. We seem to be getting too carried away with observations; our curiosity is getting the better of us. We are becoming obsessive.

Wakatta, replied Ito.

Perhaps we leave it to another day.

Another day, replied Ito. Yes, the grace of another day.

Yamatoshi Ito offered a bow to Kasuga and straightened the lining of her kimono. She ensured her obi was in place and that the napkin was well tucked in against her ribs. She lifted herself off the floor and put the two side seams of her kimono together so she could hold it firmly. She made her way to the exit, leaving the sukiya to Yamamoto Kasuga dallying with thoughts of her breast in his mouth.

Another day, Yamamoto Kasuga murmured to himself in

the quiet desolation of his mind. A tear came to his eyes and he let it drop to the floor. Another day, he murmured again as though to reassure himself that all had indeed been taken care of: the beast of his mind had been tamed and he had lived to see another day, as free as the innocence of dawn and as visceral as the hunter's choice of prey.

When the TV set regained its signal, it was to a shimmer of white noise. The image of Kasuga was pixelated in the foreground, and a smile that rested on his face seemed to suggest that all wasn't lost. In every situation, there was a fight and a call to arms; no single war was ever won without one. The gift of another day, its hours and minutes and seconds, the passage of creativity, the flight of inspiration like the lady in a crowd, and the conviction of paths having been crossed before... Christopher woke from his dreams and fell back to sleep in an instant, knowing that all was but a dream.

* * *